Subversion

A Julian Mercer novel

G.K. Parks

Copyright © 2017 G.K. Parks

A Modus Operandi imprint

All rights reserved.

ISBN: 1942710070
ISBN-13: 978-1-942710-07-3

For my mom and dad

ONE

"Sir, I must insist," Julian Mercer repeated for what felt like the millionth time, "do not harm the package."

"Then give me what I want," the unnamed voice on the other end of the line said. "I have taken control of the home and those inside. Do not test me."

"I'm working on meeting your demands." Mercer, a former Special Air Service commander, was used to dealing with difficult situations, but this current negotiation was stretching his patience. Each kidnapping and ransom was unique, but this one was downright absurd. Silently sighing, he flipped through the surveillance feed on the computer and checked the time. "We will get the money, but we need more time."

"You've been saying you need more time for the last twelve hours. Do you have the money?"

"Not yet."

"You try my patience. Perhaps you need some incentive to work faster." The sound of gunfire cut through the silence, causing Mercer to cringe. "I have the senator, his family, and his entire household staff at my disposal. I will turn this estate into a mausoleum if you do not get me my money now."

"Have they been harmed? I need proof of life."

"You'll have proof of death if you don't have a timetable for delivery in the next two minutes."

Before Mercer lost control, which was becoming increasingly likely as the minutes ticked by, he unclenched his fingers from the subconscious fist he had made. "Speak to my associate while I see what is delaying the funds." Not waiting for the kidnapper to voice a protest, Mercer unclipped the earpiece and handed it to Bastian Clarke, his second-in-command. The two men had been tag-teaming the kidnapper throughout the negotiation. "How much time?"

"Fourteen hours and counting," Bastian said before taking the call off mute.

Moving into the hallway, Mercer turned on the radio. "Donovan, I need a SitRep. He just opened fire. How many dead?"

"We heard gunshots. No indication of movement at the exterior. We have no visual. Repeat no visual. The first floor entry points and windows have been wired with explosives. We can't get close. Hans is attempting to find a second story vantage point."

"If necessary, can you breach?" Mercer asked. It wasn't a great option. There were at least twelve hostages inside and an unknown number of hostiles.

"Doubtful. It's a bloody fortress. Hans says it's impregnable." Donovan snorted. "I'll make sure he doesn't try to shag it."

Mercer let out an annoyed growl. He'd been in negotiations for the last fourteen hours, and it was starting to show. Most hostage negotiations were handled by a government agency, but kidnappings were a beast all their own. It was the family's prerogative to hire a specialist, and given Mercer's impeccable record, his team had been contacted to handle the situation quickly and quietly. The quickly part wasn't happening, and the chance of this resolving quietly was questionable.

The primary victim was a senator on holiday in the Caribbean. His privately staffed compound was surrounded on three sides by water. Reaching the estate undetected was difficult enough, which made things trickier for the K&R specialists. In order to properly scout the estate, Donovan and Hans had no choice but to enter through the main gate. As of now, they remained undetected, but that could change at any moment.

The estate's location and layout made it a security nightmare. The setup was meant to yield increased security, but now that it had been overrun by hostile forces, that same layout made it harder for help to arrive. It also drew into question exactly how the kidnapper planned to escape. With only one way out, the situation didn't bode well, and with Mercer tired and edgy, a positive resolution was even less likely.

"Find a way inside. This bastard won't listen to reason. He wants three million Euros, or he'll kill them all. We need options."

"The exterior walls on the ground floor are wired to detonate. We can try to disarm or bypass the devices," Donovan said, "but without knowing who is inside, we might be detected."

"Get the schematics to Bastian. He may know how to override the system." Focusing on the photographs pinned to the wall, Mercer narrowed his eyes. "Can you get a visual with a scope?"

"We tried, sir. The windows are covered. Hans is investigating the exterior of the upper levels. We'll let you know what we find."

"I'll stay on comms. As soon as we have entry, say the word."

"Aye." Donovan hedged before adding, "I'd suggest we find some way to have the money ready for the exchange. The disarmament looks like it might be a bit dodgy."

Reentering the room, Mercer held his hand out for the phone, and Bastian expertly maneuvered the conversation to a halt while Mercer took control again. Pointing to his watch, Bastian made sure Mercer was aware of the time crunch before returning to the computers. Some days, it'd be nice to have military resources backing their plays.

"Sir," Mercer said, "the funds are being gathered, but we will need a day."

"A day? Have I not made it clear I have a senator, his entire family, and his staff under my control?"

"You have, and I have made sure the authorities do not interfere as you dictated. If you would like this expedited, I'm sure the police or U.S. government could get you the money faster. Shall I allow them to take over?" That threat had prevailed earlier and allowed the conversation to continue, delaying the kidnapper from acting hastily.

With that many victims, a rising death toll was inevitable, but Mercer was determined to prevent that from happening. Despite what the insurance firm believed, this wasn't a kidnapping. It was a hostage situation. However, the U.S. government had no problem passing it off. It wasn't occurring on their soil, and when things went pear-shaped, they'd use Mercer as their scapegoat, blaming him for the loss of life. It was a win for the government and a loss for everyone else. The island police didn't do much of anything and weren't prepared to address a situation like this.

"No," the kidnapper said. "Do not contact the police or government. If you do, I'll kill them all."

"Fine." Mercer shifted his focus to Bastian, who was now frantically entering commands into the computer. "I'd like to remind you if any harm befalls the package, the ransom will not be paid. The money is contingent on the well-being of your captives. I need proof of life before I can proceed."

"Do you think I killed them?" The kidnapper practically laughed. "I'm sending a photo of the family with the current timestamp."

"What about the staff? You wanted me to believe you would act, and I do."

"Good."

"I need verification the staff members are alive."

"No, you don't. You were hired to negotiate the release of the senator and his family. When I start tossing bodies out the door, then you'll be certain I was not bluffing. In the meantime, you should use that fear to motivate the bank to hand over the funds in the next twelve hours, not twenty-four."

"I can't do anything to change their policies."

"Jules," Bastian whispered, "Hans came through."

Mercer leaned over the computer, getting his first glimpse inside the senator's compound. Hans had placed a fiber optic cable through a crack beneath the doorway. Four heavily armed men filled the screen. Two hostages were bound in the corner of the room. Another ten hostages and the man in charge were somewhere out of view. Unfortunately, there was no telling where they might be or how many more armed men were inside. Picking up a pen, Mercer wrote *heat signatures* and pushed the paper toward Bastian.

Bas shook his head. "They're blasting the thermostat. Thermal won't work. We tried. It's also why the windows are so foggy that we can't see inside."

"Bollocks," Mercer swore, internally cursing himself for saying that out loud. Covering, he quickly added, "The bank is suspicious of our request and is asking for additional verification. We need more time. What can I do to demonstrate our willingness to comply?"

"I want fifty thousand transferred into my account in the next five minutes, or I kill the boy," the kidnapper said, and the line went dead.

"Establish a transfer," Mercer pulled the earpiece out, "in four minutes and forty-eight seconds, and not a moment sooner. We need him to think we're scrambling."

"Aren't we?" Bastian opened another browser window and set the parameters for the transfer. "The government wants nothing to do with the situation. They don't negotiate with terrorists, and I don't think they give a shit about this bloke or his family."

"Probably not." Mercer closed his eyes and squeezed the bridge of his nose. He was exhausted. "How much are we authorized to trade?"

"Three hundred thousand, making us a bit short of the three million."

"How much do you think is inside the senator's estate?"

"Several times that. This might be his vacation home, but he owns a few masterpieces and antiquities. I'm wondering if this situation evolved out of a botched robbery. Why else would this tosser keep us on the phone so long if he just wanted a cash payout? He's buying time. I just can't be certain why," Bastian said.

"Any activity in or out?" Mercer waited for Hans or Donovan to respond.

"Negative. They're locked up tight," Donovan said.

"Then how are they planning to escape once the money transfer completes?" Mercer asked, earning a shrug from Bastian. It didn't make sense, but maybe it was the exhaustion and late hour. "What do we know so far?"

"Roughly thirty-six hours ago, a communication was sent from the compound to the senator's aide, requesting three million in exchange for the return of the senator and his staff. After verifying this wasn't a prank, the aide contacted the senator's security detail who in turn contacted the insurance company who phoned us," Bastian said. "We've spotted at least four unfriendlies inside. Then there's the shithead on the phone. That's five. And who knows how many more we can't spot."

"Bloody hell."

After receiving the call, Mercer and his team had been flown via helicopter to an airstrip with a waiting jet. Upon arriving on the island, Mercer was left to conduct business without any additional support. The only chance the team had to prep was during the flight.

"What's this wanker's motivation?"

"Possibly political, but more than likely, monetary." Bastian had skimmed Senator Harry Blaine's voting record, and while the man had made several enemies, kidnapping wasn't the way to make a political statement. Public executions and murder were the preferred methods for most terrorists and dissidents. "Jules, perhaps it's time to break the package apart and buy off the parts. I don't think we have a choice."

"I know," Mercer climbed to his feet, needing to move to keep himself alert, "but we aren't authorized to issue payouts for anyone except the senator and his immediate family. This bastard knows that. It's why he wants us on our toes and won't provide proof of life for the staff." Mercer picked up one of their spare phones. "If the kidnapper rings back, talk to him. I need to make a call."

Despite Mercer's insistence that negotiating the release of the other victims would aid in the safe return of Senator Blaine, the insurance company wouldn't listen and denied Mercer additional funds for use during the negotiation. If he wanted to free the aides and staff, so be it. But it would be on his dime.

"Knob-ends." Mercer slammed the phone down. He glanced at Bastian who was once again speaking to the kidnapper, hoping the latest payment bought them another day. Coming up with an idea, he pressed the radio. "Donovan, can you pinpoint any additional targets inside the estate using the laser mic? The kidnapper is speaking now."

"I've got the tosser," Hans said, cutting into the conversation. "Second floor, third window. No visual. If this bastard didn't steam up the place, I'd put one between his eyes. It's a bloody sauna out here. Who in their right mind would blast the heat on a day like this?"

"A fucking nutter," Donovan replied. "What do you want us to do, Jules?"

Before Mercer could respond, Bastian cleared his throat and tossed the phone onto the table. It was done. They'd been given another twenty-four hours.

"Pull back. We'll reassess," Mercer said. "Rendezvous at our secondary location. We need to safeguard our operation before we mount a rescue or conduct a face-to-face meeting."

TWO

Mercer shuffled through the papers littering the table. They had moved from the air-conditioned hotel room provided by the insurance agency to a low-budget hovel in a questionable part of the island. The move had taken over an hour, but after being double-crossed a time or two, Mercer insisted on taking every precaution to keep his teammates safe, even if it meant wasting precious time. "Aerial maps and blueprints?"

"Jules, give me a minute." Chomping down on a licorice whip, Bastian dug through the files, pulling out the images and taping them to the wall. After updating the map with a new route, he took a seat behind the computer and brought up the files. "We don't have a hard copy of the blueprint. This was e-mailed by the senator's aide. Apparently, Blaine had the estate built according to his own specifications."

"What about underground tunnels and sewer lines?" Donovan asked, helping himself to a piece of candy.

"It's a bloody island, mate," Hans chastised. "The underground is flooded. It's called the sea. Unless you're part merman, that won't get us inside."

"And it won't let them out. How did they get here?" Mercer pointed to a photograph of the estate. It was gated with a guard post and a security team on the premises. "There's no vehicle." He narrowed his eyes at the map. "One if by land, two if by sea."

"What?" Hans looked dumbfounded.

"American history. When the Yanks decided their colonies should be independent of the Crown, that was one of their signals. Never mind. Bas, we need satellite imagery of the estate from two days ago. The kidnappers must have made an aquatic landing. I want to know everything about the vessel they used to get here and where it went."

"Are your fingers broken? Give our mates at MI5 a ring. I can't do everything at once."

Mercer took a deep breath. The lack of sleep and the intense temperature change were wearing on them. Picking up the phone, he placed a call to one of their old contacts, requested the information, and hung up. Then he surveyed his team. From the looks of them, they could have been stuck in the trenches of Afghanistan for the past two days instead of a tropical paradise.

"Hans, Donovan, get some sleep. I'll let you know when we need you." Unfortunately, Bastian's skills were more valuable now than ever. Mercer couldn't dismiss his friend as easily as the two highly skilled shooters. "I'll get this mapped. Bastian will work the other angles."

Bas snorted. "Not to look a gift horse in the mouth, but what put you in such a considerate mood?"

"We need to end this, and we only have twenty-four hours. You need help, and we don't have time to squabble."

Giving Mercer a skeptical look, Bastian returned to the computer. If he could hack into the estate's security system, they might have a clear picture of what was going on inside. "Jules, does anything about this situation seem queer?"

"All of it." Mercer glanced at his friend. "That fourteen hour negotiation was meant to distract us. The kidnapper wants to keep us on a leash. Whatever's he's doing has already started."

"Are we planning a breach?"

"Only if we get eyes inside. If not, the casualties will be unacceptable. The kidnapper knows this. He knows the playbook. He might even know us."

"Are you sure that isn't the paranoia talking?"

"It bloody well might be." Settling in front of one of the other computers, Mercer opened a dialog box and reached for the list of the senator's employees. "I'll run backgrounds and see if this looks like an inside job."

"And you know how to do that?" Bastian teased, dragging his eyes away from the screen for a brief moment. "We'll have to discuss my wages one day soon since it appears you've been using me as your personal servant this entire time."

Mercer ignored the comment, entering name after name. Given that they weren't part of any government agency, access to information was limited. But Bastian had created backdoors into numerous databases. However, none of that was useful.

Professional kidnappers researched their marks, stalked their prey, and utilized whatever access was readily available. Despite the senator's enhanced security, he had a public image to maintain. That included an online calendar of events, appearances, and plenty of family photos. The man was asking for trouble.

Senator Harry Blaine had served in office for the better part of the last two decades. He was in his late forties. His wife, Barbara Blaine, affectionately referred to by adoring constituents as Bebe, was in her mid-thirties. Like her husband, she had a full and active public life. She advocated for children's literacy programs and cancer research.

Surprisingly, the two hadn't weathered any major scandals. They had one child, Nathaniel, who just turned eleven. The family had made comments and posted enough photos from previous trips to imply an impending Caribbean getaway. However, according to the itinerary, the family wasn't supposed to arrive until next week. Blaine was due to deliver an address to the servicemen, and Bebe had several dinner functions scheduled over the course of the current week. But their plans must have changed.

"Come on, darling," Bastian coaxed, "just a little more. Almost there." He tapped furiously on the keys. "Bugger." He slammed his palms on the keyboard. "Bloody firewall." Getting up, he grabbed an unopened bag of crisps and ripped open the packaging. "It'll have to be hardwired, but the hub is inside the estate. I need my gear."

"No," Mercer said.

"No?" Bas stopped halfway to the closet. "We're on a clock, Jules."

"I'm aware. But think for a moment. You can't waltz onto the grounds and hack into the security system."

"I need a bloody cigarette." Bas exhaled, hoping to calm his mind and his craving. "You're right. Something is very wrong when you're the rational one. I take it you're more accustomed to functioning under these conditions than the rest of us." He fidgeted with the bag. "Do you ever sleep?"

"When it becomes necessary." Sleep wasn't a pleasant experience. It often led to nightmares of his wife's murder or crushingly happy moments from their time together which would leave him devastated for hours afterward. "Right now, that is a luxury I cannot afford, but it appears to be a necessity for you." He nodded toward one of the empty bedrooms. "I will continue the research and devise a plan for tomorrow. We do not have the money, nor do I believe the kidnapper has any intention of surrendering the package."

"Then what are we going to do?"

"I don't know yet." Mercer studied the intel taped to the wall. "We need to identify the source of the threat and eliminate it."

Mumbling something about soldiers and wars, Bastian dropped the bag of crisps on the table and went to bed. He feared he'd wake to find Julian had abandoned the rest of the team to seek vengeance on his own. It wouldn't exactly be the first time something like that had happened. Julian was a loaded gun. It wasn't advisable to point him at a target, but that was often the case in this line of work. Still, Bas needed sleep, so he chose to trust the commander.

Left alone with his thoughts, Mercer analyzed the situation, but without any real reference points regarding the kidnapper or his motives, his efforts were awarded little progress. Closing his eyes, he visualized the estate, the security, and methods of infiltration. Like Hans said, it was a fortress, and now that the enemy was within, they were using the estate's defenses to maintain their stronghold.

Opening his eyes at the sound of the new mail notification, Mercer downloaded the satellite imagery.

Cheers, MI5, he thought. Two speedboats had circled the estate, but they never docked. However, the satellite hadn't been overhead at the time of the breach. Either the kidnapper was lucky, or he had done his research. Taking into consideration satellite positions when planning an infiltration was something unique to those involved in military strikes. That thought worried him, but until he learned more, there was no point in jumping to conclusions. But something nagged at his thoughts.

Leafing through Senator Blaine's dossier, Mercer found a few notations on Blaine's committee work dealing with armed forces and military contracts, but it wasn't detailed. He typed in a few search terms and stared at the hundreds of entries filling the screen. Growing exasperated, he closed the window. He'd leave the research to Bastian.

Instead, Mercer turned his attention back to the kidnapper. The voice on the phone belonged to a man adamantly opposed to police and government interference. If he was politically motivated, he'd want the press coverage and fanfare. This wasn't about the senator's politics. It was about something else.

What do you want, Mercer pondered. It was after four a.m., and he was out of ideas. Giving in to his physical needs, he stretched out on the sofa. They had twenty-one hours to find three million Euros or convince the kidnapper to give them more time.

THREE

"This is utter rubbish. No visual from this position either." Donovan had left the flat early to scout the grounds around the estate for another method of entry, but his search came up empty. A breach wasn't possible. "Any luck from the other side?"

"Negative," Hans replied into his comm. "The bird who rented me the boat offered to take me around and show me the sights. I would have had better luck seeing her sights than anything inside this bloody mansion."

"No visual," Mercer repeated, hoping to keep their communication succinct. "Any movement to report?"

"Negative, sir," Hans said, which Donovan echoed.

"Jules," Bastian said from behind his computer, "if you can get me close enough, I'll splice into the estate's CCTVs. At least we'll get a look inside."

"I wouldn't recommend it," Donovan said. "The security station monitors the feed, but the kidnappers cut the cables. The only access left isn't on ground level, making a retreat impossible if you're spotted."

Mercer blew out a breath. "Hold position. Maintain

radio silence unless there is unusual activity to report."

"Aye," Hans said.

"Yes, sir," Donovan added.

The slight static buzz from Mercer's earpiece quieted. He switched it to mute and paced the expanse of their command center, studying the photo array taped to the wall. They couldn't look inside. They couldn't use any of their high-tech toys to determine how many hostiles and hostages were within the confines of the house. And they were running out of time.

"You should let me go. Frankly, you shouldn't have stopped me last night when I was far more gung-ho about the prospect," Bas said. "Lack of sleep leads to poor judgment. Shit, you probably could have convinced me to knock on the front door and tell them I was the cable guy."

"It's too dangerous for the hostages and for you." Mercer looked down at the phone, daring it to ring. "I'll insist on the exchange in person. It should buy us more time and get us close enough to determine the situation."

"That's assuming the kidnapper agrees and allows you onto the property. I don't see either of those things happening."

"If he wants the cash, I won't give him a choice." The suitcase in the corner held only a fraction of the ransom. "The trick will be getting him to agree to engage in separate negotiations for each of the hostages. Do you have profiles on the senator's staff yet?"

"Here." Bas handed Mercer the files. "Didn't you say you weren't authorized to negotiate the separate release of the staff members?"

"What choice do we have? Should I let them

perish?"

Bastian fell silent. Their requests for additional proof of life were never answered. The house staff and the senator's aides may already be dead. The attempt to negotiate their releases might turn into a fruitless endeavor or a tragic one. The situation was difficult to gauge, and a single question nagged at Bastian. Finally, he said, "I don't know how this will end. If we are correct in believing this was a botched burglary, wouldn't the kidnapper take his spoils and leave the senator and his family behind?"

"Perhaps."

"Do you think he murdered the staff?"

Mercer shrugged.

"Julian, controlling that many hostages for any length of time would be difficult, even if there are five armed men inside the house. Killing one of the captives would earn compliance from those who remain."

"Don't you think I realize that? The longer this drags on, the more casualties we'll encounter, but without the three million, we have to delay."

Thoughts swam through Mercer's mind. The pieces weren't joining together in a way that would complete the picture. Instead, they were leading down a wayward path. Grabbing a pen, he circled the estate, flipped through the employee dossiers, pinned the staff photos to the wall, and studied the map of the island. Island natives would know the best way to navigate the waters and the streets. The local police weren't privy to the senator's blight, but they might be aware of strangers lurking about.

"Ring the bobbies," Mercer said. "Tell them we are working private security for the senator and need to know if they've flagged any suspicious activity."

"What if they want our credentials?"

"Make them look good."

"Fine, but don't forget to fetch me from jail."

While Bastian made the call, Mercer analyzed the list of staff on the premises at the time of the takeover. The kidnapper hadn't provided a headcount or names, leaving them with a bit of guesswork. That tactic made it easier to mask insider involvement and disguise potential unfriendlies as hostages if the situation escalated into a tactical maneuver. Thankfully, the senator's staff who remained in the States had provided a list of aides who had traveled with the family and a list of personal employees on the senator's payroll who were responsible for maintaining the vacation home. Mercer estimated twelve hostages in addition to the Blaines, bringing the total to fifteen victims.

Selecting which victim to free first could help resolve this quickly and easily. The kidnapper would be less likely to barter with the lives of Harry, Barbara, or Nathaniel Blaine for anything less than three million. So it was time to decide which of the staffers would provide the most use.

Mercer's first choice was the groundskeeper. He would be able to provide valuable intel on the layout of the home. Security personnel was a close second, but it was a roll of the dice. The constraints of Blaine's insurance policy limited Mercer's options.

He dropped his pen and spun around to face Bastian. "You mean to tell me Blaine is worth millions and his ransom insurance is only three hundred thousand? Someone's screwing with us."

"I'll make a call," Bastian offered. After several minutes, a few uh-huhs, and numerous curses, he hung up. "The senator didn't even want the insurance, but by getting it, he lowered his premiums elsewhere. Why is it the rich will do anything to save a few quid?

He must not have expected this to happen, or he figured he had enough money to write a check and get himself out of trouble."

"Prat."

Lifting the phone, Mercer dialed and waited. After three rings, the same voice he had spoken to the prior day answered. The kidnapper offered no greeting. He didn't sound nearly as needy or talkative. That didn't bode well for the negotiation.

"Do you have the money?"

"Not all of it," Mercer said. "We're in the process of collecting the funds."

"You're almost out of time. You don't want to see what happens if you fail to follow through."

"Need I remind you if anything befalls the senator or his family, the ransom will not be paid," Mercer said, feeling like a broken record. "However, I'd like to propose a new trade."

"What do you want?"

"How many of the senator's staff are you holding?"

"Twelve."

That was progress. "I'd like to negotiate the release of as many as possible."

"À la carte?" The kidnapper chuckled. "This isn't a restaurant."

"You are contained in a known location with only one escape route. You must be outmanned with that many hostages. I'm offering to give you what you want and make this situation easier. There's no reason everyone can't walk away breathing."

"Give me five minutes."

The phone went dead, and Mercer dropped the receiver. He tore through the blueprints and maps. This guy had an escape plan, but Mercer had no idea what it was.

"Y'know, this really isn't our area of expertise,"

Bastian mused. "This is a hostage situation. The hostiles are pinned down inside a building. They are armed and holding over a dozen potential victims. This could easily turn into a bloodbath if we don't tread lightly. Jules, we're out of our depth."

"We've rectified hostage situations before. This is no different."

"This is completely different. This isn't an enemy encampment with POWs. We don't have air support. We don't have snipers' nests. We don't have a secondary SpecOps team waiting to advance."

"We could position our snipers." Mercer pointed to the aerial map. "Figure out where Hans and Donovan should set up."

"That's not what I meant. The coppers would be better equipped to handle this."

"What did they say when you phoned?"

"Nothing. Someone has to verify my identity, and then they'll get back to me."

"You can't expect lazy wankers like that to be prepared for a situation like this. This is an island, mate. The coppers deal with tourists' complaints of being swindled. In case you haven't noticed, outside our door are a lot of sketchy types. Dealers, mainly. From the condition of things around here, the police turn a blind eye to the drug problem, and they let the natives fend for themselves. It's doubtful they even give two shits about the tourists if they wander too far from the resorts and hotels."

"I don't believe that's entirely accurate."

Before Mercer could launch into another anti-police rant, the phone rang. The five minutes were up. Taking a moment to quiet his mind and neutralize his emotions, he inhaled deeply and answered the phone.

"I've decided you're correct. We should lighten the load," the kidnapper said. Without asking for payment or negotiating a release, he hung up.

"Shit," Hans' voice broke through the radio silence, "we have movement. A bloody lot. The whole bloody lot."

"I need a visual," Mercer said to Bastian, who was already behind the computer doing whatever he could to get a current satellite image of the estate. "Hans, report."

"They marched them out. Four armed men and what appears to be ten hostages."

"Donovan?" Mercer asked, hoping for confirmation.

"I can't see anything from this location. Repositioning."

"My god," Hans swore. The sound of rifle fire echoed in the background. "These bastards are having them walk the literal plank."

"Hans, intercept," Mercer ordered. "Return fire. Minimize civilian casualties. Donovan, provide ground support."

"I'm on my way," Donovan replied while Mercer and Bastian listened to the echo of gunfire and Hans' curses.

"The hostages are in the water," Hans said. "I've lost visual on the enemy. They retreated inside while firing on the hostages. Advise. Do we attempt a breach?"

"Fish them out," Bastian said. "I can't get a view of the estate. Donovan any movement on your side of the property?"

"Nothing. No movement. Repeat no movement. The front is secure. I'm moving around to the side to get a partial visual of the back. So far, no hostiles present."

"Hans, what's their condition?" Mercer asked.

"Almost there." Hans gunned the boat's engine.

"They appear to be unharmed." The rumble of the engine cut out, and Hans called to them. "They've been shackled together and thrust into the water. There's a deep drop from the shallow beach. If enough drown, they all drown."

"Get them out of there, quick pace," Bastian instructed. "Rescue and retreat."

Before Mercer could do anything, the phone rang.

"You wanted the hostages. Now you have them. Most of them. I'm keeping the senator, his wife, and his son unless you deliver three million Euros. The original timeframe stands. And one other thing, tell your man to leave the boat docked on the property or things will become unpleasant for the family. A change of venue is in order." The line went dead, and Mercer cursed.

"More good news?" Bastian asked.

"We've been played."

FOUR

"I deposited the boat," Hans said, "Luckily, we managed to hitch a ride with some local fishermen. They called the authorities, who should be arriving soon. The hostages are with Donovan now. I'm circling back to see if I can keep tabs on the hostiles."

"Watch your arse. I'm on my way." Mercer checked to make sure his weapon was secured in its holster and picked up the business card and credentials Bastian created. "This tosser plans to use the hostage release as a way to distract us while he runs. They must know we don't have another watercraft at our disposal, and by the time we get one, they'll be gone. We fucked this up."

"Jules," Bastian said, "he made certain we didn't have enough time to adequately plan. I'll stay here and do my best to track their movements. The speedboat might have an onboard navigation system. If it does, I'll hack into it. Now go."

Climbing into one of the three rental vehicles, Mercer drove away. The waterlogged victims might be able to provide useful information. He needed to speak to the hostages before the authorities did.

Slamming on the brakes, he left the vehicle parked along the side of the road. Very few vehicles actually used the streets. Instead, most people took advantage of the warm, beachy climate to walk and sightsee. Even the residents found it easier to maneuver about on foot.

The fishermen had dropped the lot off at an outdoor market. Donovan had intercepted them. Presently, the coppers weren't on scene, but that would change within the next few minutes. Spotting Donovan, Mercer headed for him while scanning the area for possible threats.

A group of drenched, harried individuals remained bound together, sitting in a long row against the back of one of the stands.

"Several have contusions. Two were grazed. I offered assistance, but they won't speak. They didn't like me poking around so close to them, so I backed off. You might want to give it a go before the police and ambulances arrive. They must speak English, given their employer, but who knows," Donovan said.

Mercer moved closer to the group. Handcuffs bound one person's ankle to another person's ankle in a human daisy chain. They had to move as a unit. Swimming must have been difficult, if not damn near impossible. It was a miracle Hans had managed such a swift recovery. Perhaps the kidnapper planned to use the mass drowning as a distraction to escape. Mercer snorted, pleased that some part of the kidnapper's plan had been foiled.

"Does anyone need immediate medical assistance?" he asked.

A couple of people shook their heads, but no one looked up.

"I'm Julian Mercer. My associate Hans was on the boat." He jerked his head toward Donovan while he swept the crowd for a sign of acknowledgement or recognition. "That's my other associate, Donovan. We were hired to negotiate your release."

No one said anything, but Mercer couldn't help but get hung up on the headcount. Ten hostages, not twelve. He crouched down, studying each of their faces and trying to recall who was missing. A security guard and one of the maids, perhaps.

"Was anyone left behind?" Mercer asked. "Was anyone killed?"

A woman near the middle curled in on herself. A couple of people near her grew increasingly antsy, but no one spoke. The kidnapper said he was only keeping the family for ransom. Either the bastard lied, or he had murdered two people.

"He can't hurt you. You are safe now," Mercer said. "But I need you to answer my questions."

Donovan stepped closer, whispering in Mercer's ear, "Take it easy. They appear to be under some sort of duress."

"We don't have time for this." Calming his tone, he addressed the group again. "The police will be here shortly. They will see to it you receive the care and treatment you need. But I need to know what's going on. What did the kidnapper want?" No one answered. "At some point one of you will have to speak to someone."

Donovan edged closer at the sound of incoming sirens. "We have company."

"Did he release you all?" Mercer asked. "I was informed there should be twelve, not ten of you." He studied their expressions, but aside from a few uneasy twitches and blinks, no one acknowledged him. "You have nothing to fear. We won't hurt you. You are safe.

We want to stop the men responsible for this. Did he ask any of you to speak on his behalf? Is he doing something to you right now to prevent you from speaking to us? We will protect you."

A few cast their eyes toward the middle of the chain. It was impossible to determine precisely where their focus went, but that gesture didn't go unnoticed.

Mercer snorted, hoping to goad one of them into speaking. "Apparently, you served no purpose and didn't warrant a list of demands. The kidnapper's only request was three million Euros in exchange for the senator and his family."

It was the perfect opportunity for someone to come forward and deliver additional demands, but no one did. Several doors slammed, and the police announced themselves. Regardless of location, it always sounded the same.

Out of time and throwing caution to the wind, Mercer went with his gut, deciding the most logical reason for their silence was an infiltrator in their midst. "I know one of you is working with the kidnapper. It'd be in your best interest to identify yourself now because once we find you, things will not be pleasant."

No one moved.

"That's the same amount of progress I made," Donovan muttered. "I'll keep an eye on them while you update the bobbies."

Mercer dreaded what was about to happen. He loathed the police. They had failed him when he needed them most, and they repeatedly failed him every time he was forced to work alongside them during these ransom negotiations. The cops had no idea what was at stake or how to practice finesse, not that Mercer was much better at that particular feat, but he and his team knew what drove men to act and acknowledged that fulfilling their desires often led to positive outcomes. The police didn't have the same guidelines. They wanted to punish the offenders, and often, the victims were harmed in the process.

"Julian Mercer." Mercer extended his hand to the nearest officer. "I was hired to provide security for the senator and his staff. Unfortunately, when I arrived, I found the estate had been breached by an unknown number of armed men." He handed the skeptical cop his credentials. "My team and I have been in negotiation with these scoundrels. However, they acted unexpectedly. Several of the staff have been injured." He lowered his voice, knowing the police officer didn't believe a word he said. "The senator and his family have been kidnapped, and at least one of them," he jerked his thumb at the group, "is working with the kidnapper. They aren't speaking. I'll need full profiles of the victims after they have been questioned and copies of any statements they provide. A few require medical attention. Make sure you see to that."

The cop scratched his head, watching as his colleagues unshackled the victims and ushered the uninjured into waiting vehicles. "Your identity will have to be verified. Until then, stay where I can see you. The captain will address your issues." He handed Mercer's credentials to another officer and went to assist the triage efforts.

Mercer watched the scene unfold, paying close attention to the nosy onlookers gathered around the police cars. One, in particular, was filming on his phone.

"Donovan, handle that. I need to figure out what's going on. Hans might have something useful to share. Bas is in charge of the negotiation until I get back."

"You're staying here?"

"We have no choice." Mercer watched as the last

handcuff was removed from the final victim's ankle.

"Do you actually believe one of the victims is a wolf in sheep's clothing?"

"Possibly." Mercer adjusted his sunglasses. "If not, they were on the inside. They can help."

"Only if they start speaking. You don't think their tongues have been cut out, do you?"

"Stop." But they'd seen that happen in a few smaller provinces. It was a common punishment for traitors.

"Mr. Mercer," a voice called from the other side of the square, and Mercer spun to see a sharply dressed man with aviator sunglasses approaching, "I believe your colleague phoned earlier. I'm Captain Caho. It seems we have a problem."

"Go on."

"Our tiny island is accustomed to dealing with celebrities and the things that follow—paparazzi, obsessed fanatics, the occasional stalker. However, most of the rich and powerful come here because the seclusion provides a sanctuary. Privacy is easily obtained." He took off his sunglasses and hung them from his open collar. "How did this happen?"

"You tell me."

"You are in charge of security, no?"

"I arrived after the situation escalated."

"Of course." Caho glanced at the departing fleet of police cars and the stragglers vacating the square. "What can you tell me about the victims?"

"They are part of the senator's staff. I believe one of them is working with the kidnapper."

"Why?"

"They won't speak. No one voiced a complaint or even a whisper of gratitude. Typically, victims express some emotion."

"I see." Caho reached into his pocket and removed

a notepad and pen. "Do you have photos and employee records of the staff members in question?"

"Yes."

"May I have them?"

"They'll be forwarded to your office. I'd appreciate it if you would share the information you garner from the victims with me, since they wouldn't respond to my questions."

"They have no reason to speak to you. You let them get kidnapped." Caho put his sunglasses back on. "How long have you served the senator?"

"I just started."

"You probably shouldn't expect a promotion." Caho chuckled. "Do you need assistance in planning a rescue? If so, I can contact the consulate and have this sorted out. However, I've been warned not to interfere."

"By whom?"

"You, of course. Or your people." He waved the thought away as if it were an annoying gnat. "Is there something you would like me to do?"

Perplexed by the odd nature of the question and the standoffish attitude of the police captain, Mercer chose to err on the side of caution. "Have you noticed anything strange related to the senator's most recent visit?"

"I've rarely encountered the man. Whenever he visits the island, he stays on his property. He's never gone to any of our shops or restaurants. He's never taken a moment to sightsee. He could be vacationing here at any time, and no one would know. That estate, the private beach, and surrounding grounds are that man's island unto himself. You'll have difficulty finding anyone who can help in your quest to rescue him. I wish you luck, my friend." Handing back Mercer's credentials, Caho turned and headed toward a luxury sedan parked on the far end of the market. Compared to the rest of the vehicles, it stuck out like a sore thumb.

FIVE

Mercer returned to the flat to find Bastian on the phone. The kidnapper had called again. Mercer reached for the phone, but Bas shook his head and jerked his chin toward the back room where Hans was updating their dossiers.

"We blew our load prematurely," Hans griped. "They must have made us. Judging from what I saw, this bastard wanted me close enough to intervene. With the exterior cameras, they had a bloody brilliant view of the water. I should have been more careful and used a quieter vessel. I just thought it would have been less conspicuous to go for a joyride than sneak around."

"What do we know?"

"Four armed men hauled the entire lot outside. They marched them out in a line. I had no idea they were shackled together. Gunfire erupted. At first, I thought these bastards were gunning them all down, but the shots went high. A couple of bullets glanced off one or two of them. I didn't even realize it until I fished them out. If they were hoping to attract sharks, they needed more carnage to chum the waters."

"Where did the gunmen go?"

"By the time I brought the boat around, they vanished. Since they didn't cross paths with Donovan, they must have retreated back into that fortress. There's a glass sliding door at the back of the house to facilitate beach access. I believe that's where they came from and where they went. But they have the door blacked out, and with the heaters running full blast, there was no way to get a thermal view inside." Hans dropped the pen onto the table. "These arseholes even took our boat."

"Did it have a nav system?"

"No. Bas already asked. He contacted the rental shop to see about GPS trackers and lowjacks, but that's a fool's errand. They either sunk it, or they're long gone. How are we supposed to track them now? There are a million unmapped islands nearby."

Storming back into the main room, Mercer watched Bastian jot down a few notes. The phone was on the table.

"The price just went up," Bastian said. "Five million Euros. This wanker believes two million for ten hostages is more than adequate, and since he already delivered, we should plan to do the same shortly. However, until he gets settled, a bit more time's been added to the clock."

"Are we positive the senator and his family are alive?" Mercer asked.

"Aye. We've received a video. From the footage, I'd say they are on the speedboat. I've called the local coast guard to search for our watercraft, but it's unlikely it will be spotted. There are dozens of these rentals around the islands." Bastian chomped down on a carrot stick. "How are the hostages? Is everyone alive?"

"They aren't speaking. They're terrified, but I can't figure out why. The police should be able to assist, but something doesn't smell right."

"It's all the fish and the sea air," Hans said.

"Donovan snapped a shot of the police captain and his vehicle," Bastian said. "I'm working on his profile, but I believe your distrust has more to do with his position than anything else."

Mercer surveyed the room. "Where is Donovan?"

"He's having a chat with our camera happy friend," Bastian said. "He's using our hotel room to conduct the interrogation. It shouldn't take long."

"Good." Mercer rubbed his sore shoulder, a remnant from a previous interrogation. "Have you contacted the insurance firm to update them on the situation?"

"Just about to."

"Find out if we can get an advance on the account maximum. We're going to need it. I don't give a shit about authorization." Mercer turned to Hans. "Grab your gear. We're storming the castle."

* * *

"It's the dog's bollocks," Hans whispered in reverence. "Shite, why don't we move our operating base here?"

Mercer glanced warily up the staircase. Gesturing for the younger man to stay put in the event they had company, Mercer ventured deeper into the expansive first floor. It was the ideal vacation getaway. Anyone would be more than happy to come here for holiday. The architecture and décor were minimalist modern, but the few pieces of artwork that dotted the home were expensive masterpieces. Nothing had been touched. Perhaps this wasn't a robbery gone awry.

Turning a corner, Mercer entered the dining room. The glass table had been turned into a pile of jagged pieces on the hardwood floor. The chairs were askew, overturned and scattered about, and the crystal serving pieces were broken in the side cabinet.

The kitchen appeared untouched, but the staff would have been the only ones to use the room. Mercer opened the refrigerator door with gloved hands. The items inside appeared fresh. Nothing was expired or moldy. The knives and other cookware were in order.

The living room, drawing room, and library were just as pristine as the kitchen. This estate could be a museum with the artwork, antiquities, and the clean, unused appearance. The laundry room and maid's quarters were in the far east corner. Neither looked like they belonged in the same house. They were tiny and cluttered.

Finding a flip phone beneath the mattress, Mercer attempted to power it on, but it was dead. Pocketing the device, he checked the drawers and cabinets but found nothing else of interest.

"After you." Hans stepped back, gesturing for Mercer to go up the stairs. "Did you find anything?"

"A struggle occurred in the dining room."

"Goody, a game of *Clue*."

"Shh." Mercer held up a hand, halting their procession and straining to hear movement from the floor above.

Rolling his eyes and letting out an audible sigh, Hans took to leaning against the banister.

"Hans," Mercer hissed sharply, "shh."

Gesturing that Hans explore the rooms to the right, Mercer took the rooms to the left. Several bedrooms and a theater room comprised the second floor. After performing a cursory evaluation of the bedrooms and finding nothing of use, Mercer went in search of Hans.

The sharpshooter was kneeling on the floor of a child's bedroom. The mattress was askew. The window coverings hung in a state of disarray. A hell of a fight had broken out in here.

"Blood." Hans pointed to the smears. "Someone was hurt." He looked around the room. "This is the boy's bedroom. Jules, I don't like this."

Mercer examined the bloodstain that soaked through the carpeting and the smears of red that covered the edges of the bedclothes and a few of the drawers. "We've received proof of life. The boy's well."

Hans stood, working his jaw muscles. "He's alive. That doesn't mean he's well. These tossers have no qualms about hurting innocent people. What did they even want? They could have snagged one of the paintings from downstairs and been done with it."

"Have you finished searching the rest of the rooms?"

"Not yet."

Mercer continued to the next room. A few beds were unmade, but nothing was out of the ordinary. For a family of three, they had a lot of bedrooms. Of course, the house staff and the senator's professional staff would need places to sleep too, and the maid's quarters weren't large enough to hold a dozen people.

Ending the search in the master suite, Mercer was drawn to the opened wall safe. The kidnapper probably already had whatever he wanted. "Bugger."

Removing his phone, he took a few snapshots of the safe and sent them to Bastian. Having the make and model would link back to when the safe was purchased and installed. It would probably be another dead end, but it was worth exploring. Everything at this point was.

Muffled footfalls shuffled into the room. Mercer

turned to see Hans eyeing the space heaters aimed at the windows. They were off, but the temperature inside was still a balmy ninety degrees, having barely dropped from what must have been a hundred degrees a few hours earlier.

"The heat's rather unpleasant," Hans said. "Oppressive, like the kidnapper and the assault team he brought with him." Crossing the room to the automated security system, Hans removed the front panel, spliced a few wires, and connected an external device to it. Then he dialed Bastian for further instructions on accessing the feed and the recorded footage. "Jules, we need you at the guard post. Bas will unlock the system from here so I can get the actual drives, but the manual override is outside. It'd be best if our sabotaging the system doesn't alert the authorities."

"On my way."

SIX

"I want proof of life and photographs of your captives," Mercer demanded, the phone pressed to his ear. "Further negotiations will cease until you provide proof." He hung up. "Play the video again."

Bastian tapped a button, and the video the kidnapper sent earlier played on the screen. It was a brief shot of the senator, his wife, and their son. From the angle, it was impossible to tell the condition of any of them. The camera focused heavily on Senator Harry Blaine. He looked downright annoyed, but he didn't appear injured. Barbara was sitting sideways with Nathaniel's face cradled against her chest. Her cheek was swollen. For all Mercer knew, she might have had an icepick through the other side of her skull. And then there was Nathaniel. He kept his face buried against his mother. If the scene at the house was any indication, the child had been harmed, but it was impossible to tell the extent of his injuries or the direness of their situation.

"The dining room and boy's room were destroyed,"

Hans said, taking a seat beside Bastian. He picked through the blueprints, scribbling notes on the way each room had been left.

"Have you made any progress on the cell phone?" Bas asked.

"It's charging. As soon as there's enough juice to power it on, I'll run down the number, go through the contacts, messages, recent calls, and get our mates in military intelligence to work some magic." Hans looked around the room. "Did Donovan come back yet?"

"No. Do you think that's odd?"

"It depends on what that paparazzo wanker had to say." Mercer stalked across the room, rifling through the paperwork until he found the printed files on the safe. It was top of the line, requiring a six digit code in addition to fingerprint recognition. If the senator still possessed all his digits, he was a lucky man. "What do you think the kidnapper wants? There are millions of dollars in artwork untouched inside. His motivation can't be financial."

"Fencing stolen merchandise takes contacts, patience, and a bit of luck. Ransoming his captives is riskier, but it may have been easier," Bastian said.

"Not when it comes to dealing with Jules," Hans retorted with a smile.

The phone rang, and Mercer steeled himself for whatever was to come. Most of the time, kidnappers would comply with the proof of life request. But sometimes, just asking could backfire. Hoping Bastian would be able to conduct a trace and get GPS coordinates for the kidnapper's location, Mercer waited for the go-ahead before answering the call.

"A photo will be sent to your phone. However, I would like to make it clear I do not appreciate being questioned," the kidnapper said.

"I cannot negotiate unless I have verification the senator and his family are healthy," Mercer said. Bastian spun his hand in the air, hoping Julian could keep the conversation going. "Violence will not guarantee your demands are met. In fact, it might impede the negotiation. I caution you against injuring any of the parties. We are prepared to meet your demands as quickly and efficiently as possible."

"That's funny, Mr. Mercer," the kidnapper said. "You have yet to do anything quickly or efficiently. Here's the photo. And don't waste time tracing this call. I'm using a SAT phone. Your tricks and deception will not work here. I will call back in an hour for a progress report on the five million. Perhaps you should spend that time preparing another feasible lie."

The line went dead, and Mercer slammed his palm against the desk with enough force to shake the floor. They needed access to the senator's staff. They needed to ferret out the mole.

The phone chimed, and Mercer opened the file. As was evident in the video, Blaine appeared healthy, but Barbara had been slapped around. Nathaniel had taken the brunt of the abuse. He put up as much of a fight as a child could. A long gash ran from his scalp to his cheek. His lip was split, and his shoulder was bruised.

Hans peered over Julian's shoulder. "Those bastards knocked him into the edge of the dresser. It's about damn time someone knock them into something or off the side of a cliff."

"Jules?" Bastian knew Mercer well enough to worry what course of action his friend planned to take.

"I'm going to see what's keeping Donovan. Should he ring back, I expect you will handle things. What did the insurance company say?"

"They'll consider our request to empty the entire account and offer us an advance based on Blaine's collateral, but they capped the total at 1.6 million Euros. We're short, and nothing about our previous communications indicates the kidnapper will come down in price."

"It isn't about the money," Hans said. "If it were, he would have emptied out the mansion. However, I'd wager that's precisely what we should do. We can find some fences and gather as much as we can."

"It'll take too long. And in the event things go sideways, it implicates us," Bastian said.

"In that case, I'll head to the hospital and see if I can get the staffers to speak to me." Hans made eye contact with Mercer. "If someone gives me a hard time, I'll shoot him."

"Okay." Without waiting for Bastian's protest, Mercer left for the hotel.

It was only after several quick turns that Mercer realized his fingers were cramped around the steering wheel. Under normal conditions, he was tightly wound, but the lack of sleep and constant annoyances had left him edgy and irritated. More so than usual, anyway. A child was hurt. A woman was taken. And after all the negotiating, he still didn't possess the slightest shred of information about the person responsible. He didn't even have an alias by which to refer to the kidnapper.

Sliding into a spot near the hotel, Mercer waited inside the car, paying close attention to the other vehicles that drove by. No one was following him, but he couldn't help but think that was because the kidnapper had already escaped.

Getting out of the car, he went straight into the hotel, pressed the button for the lift, and waited. He felt eyes on him. Turning his head and coughing, he spotted the desk clerk watching him. A man sat in a chair in the lobby, reading the paper, but Mercer wasn't certain he wasn't tracking his every move.

Once the lift arrived, Mercer walked away, turned left, and took the stairs up. Out of habit, he exited on the next level, pressed the elevator call button, and returned to the staircase.

No one was in the fourth floor hallway, but Mercer kept his head down, aware of the security cameras. He slid the room key through the slot, waited for the light to turn green, and twisted the knob.

"It's me," Mercer bellowed, hoping to avoid any unpleasantness with the business end of Donovan's firearm. However, his greeting was met with silence. Locking the door, he realized the security bar hadn't been on. Surely, he had trained his people better than that. "Donovan?" Mercer cleared his gun from the holster beneath his jacket.

The suite was pristine. The living room and kitchenette were spotless. Checking the master bedroom, Mercer didn't spot anything amiss. The secondary bedroom was equally tidy. Perhaps housekeeping had already been here. Reaching for the bathroom doorknob, Mercer caught the faintest whiff of sunscreen and cologne. Something spicy with undertones of coconut and vanilla. Someone besides Mercer and his team had been inside the room.

"Donovan?"

A strangled moan came from inside the bathroom. Leaning against the wall, Mercer twisted the doorknob. He raised his gun while keeping his body to the side of the doorway. He pushed the door open slowly, edging it wider with the tip of his shoe. Frantic grunts sounded from within, and Mercer pushed the door harder.

A shotgun blasted through the partially opened

door, and a muffled scream followed. Luckily, Mercer's position protected him from the buckshot. Ducking against the decimated doorframe, he aimed around the corner, finding the shotgun on the floor. A tripwire had caused the weapon to discharge. The remnants of the trap remained on the floor next to a bound, gagged, and wide-eyed Donovan.

"Bloody fantastic." Mercer's pulse pounded. He knelt beside his teammate and ripped the duct tape from Donovan's mouth. Anger and relief fought for control of his vocal cords. "How did you let this happen?"

"They were waiting for us." Donovan rubbed the back of his head and winced. "I'm sorry, commander."

"Don't be sorry. Who were they? What did they want?"

Donovan took the offered towel, pressing it against his bleeding scalp. "I don't know. I didn't see it coming. The room looked just as we left it, so I brought that guy inside and dragged him into the bathroom, figuring the fear of drowning might loosen his lips after what the kidnappers did to the staff. But someone was waiting in the loo."

Mercer opened the separate door to the toilet cautiously, not wanting to risk a repeat of another shotgun blast. But nothing happened. The smell of sunscreen and cologne grew exponentially stronger. Whoever the offender was, he had been lying in wait.

Crumpled behind the door was a body riddled with bullets. The lack of blood meant one thing. He had been killed elsewhere and brought here.

Mercer recognized the dead man as one of Blaine's security guards. That left only one maid unaccounted for. He knelt closer, inhaling deeply, but the dead man was not the source of the sunscreen cologne stench.

"Where's our captive?"

"I don't know." Donovan stared at the ground. "I came to right before the fireworks started." He blinked against the dizziness. "Surely, someone heard the blast."

"Grab the laundry bag. Perhaps Bastian can pull something useful from the weapon." The next problem was deciding how to handle the deceased.

Donovan reached behind the door, removing the white opaque plastic bag. Before either man could make another move, knocking sounded at the door.

"Fucking hell." Donovan looked around, realizing there was no way to hide what happened. Another knock and an announcement followed. "Bloody hotel security. They're coming in."

"Let's go," Mercer said.

It'd be impossible to explain the weapon discharge and the body, and being arrested and questioned would impede negotiations which was probably what the kidnapper had in mind. The security bar on the door would buy them a few seconds. Mercer raced into the main room, grasping the door handle just as the telltale unlock beep sounded. He held the knob tightly, fighting against the guard outside who was attempting entry.

When the lock reengaged, Mercer released the handle and dashed back to Donovan. Thankfully, they had mapped an escape route from the terrace, but they had to leave now. Donovan reached for the shotgun, but Mercer grabbed his arm.

"There's no time. Go." Shoving Donovan toward the balcony, Mercer cast a final glance at the suite door just as it opened, locking in place several centimeters later when the security bar reached its limit.

"Sir, open up," the hotel employee bellowed.

Mercer went onto the balcony and waited for Donovan to drop to the terrace below. The recon specialist landed with catlike stealth but teetered and grabbed the guardrail to regain his balance. Vaulting over the railing, Mercer lowered himself down the side, swung his legs forward, and dropped, landing beside Donovan.

"After you," Donovan said, needing to hold the rail to stabilize himself. Another three drops and they'd be on ground level, but he wasn't certain he would make it.

"Forget it." Mercer gave the terrace door handle a twist, surprised when it popped open. "We'll do this the easy way." Pushing into the third floor room, Mercer marched past the elderly couple wearing Bermuda shorts and matching flowered tops and out the main door. "Take the stairs and go out the service entrance. I'll meet you there."

Pressing the button for the lift, Mercer waited for the doors to open. Then he pressed the button for the lobby. Forty seconds later, he stepped out. The man with the newspaper was gone, and the desk clerk was on the phone. Mercer went through the front door, scanned the area, and looped around the block, rendezvousing with Donovan near the rear exit.

"This was no botched robbery. This kidnapping is a calculated move. We need to get to Hans. Are you functional?" Mercer asked.

"Yes, sir." Donovan tossed the bloody towel into the dumpster and followed Mercer back to the car.

SEVEN

"What happened to you?" Hans asked.

Without answering, Donovan rubbed the back of his skull, checking to see that the bleeding had stopped. He wasn't used to being the center of attention. He dealt in reconnaissance and long-range tactics. Being up close and personal with these pricks wasn't necessarily on his to-do list, particularly if he was the one being assaulted.

"Any progress?" Mercer's eyes roved over the sparsely populated emergency room. The last time Mercer had stepped foot inside a hospital, a horrific shootout occurred, leaving several dead. Under these circumstances, the environment was giving him a bad feeling.

"The police have the victims locked up tight. I've been working Nurse Veronica. She's this close to sneaking me in to speak to my uncle, Fernando, but she got called away to perform rounds. So I'm waiting," Hans said.

"She bought that?" Donovan asked.

"Why, mate? Don't I look like I could have an Uncle Fernando? You know he was Senator Blaine's groundskeeper. Poor man, taken hostage by a team of psychopaths, nearly shot to pieces, and then almost drowned."

"Enough," Mercer said. "We're being observed. Targeted."

"By whom?" Hans asked.

"I don't know," Donovan said. "I was jumped."

"Seriously?" Hans asked. "Shit. Why didn't they just kill you?"

"They used him as bait," Mercer said. "Tripwire and a shotgun."

"Old school." Hans focused on the bored-looking officers stationed outside the patient rooms. "Perhaps we should report it. Think you can ham it up a bit?"

"Jules?" Donovan asked.

They didn't have time to waste, but it might give the police something else to pursue while they resolved the kidnapping. And whenever the police were notified of the situation inside their hotel room, it would provide an effective alibi, assuming they needed one.

Nodding, Mercer went to speak to the officers. He turned and pointed to Donovan, and one of the officers crossed the room.

"Now's your chance to see dear old Fernando." Donovan braced himself for the barrage of questions as Hans slipped away.

Forty-five minutes later, Mercer and Donovan finished speaking to the police. Donovan had told them how he'd been jumped by at least one assailant, possibly more, and conked on the head. The rest of the details he conveniently left out.

"You can file a report at the station," the officer

said. "Was anything stolen?" Donovan hadn't been carrying an ID, and the cash on his person remained. Even his side arm hadn't been removed. Whoever did this had been in a rush.

"No, sir."

"Did you see anything, Mr. Mercer?" the officer asked.

"No. I was worried when my friend didn't return and went looking for him."

"It was fortunate you located him so quickly. This isn't a big island, but people occasionally go missing."

"He wasn't missing. He was attacked," Mercer said. "I thought after this morning the police might have us under surveillance. Perhaps someone saw something. Perhaps one of your colleagues took a few liberties."

"No, sir." The officer glanced back at his partner. "Like I said, you can file a report at the station."

"Thanks," Donovan said.

Mercer nodded to Hans who had stepped out of the hospital room twenty minutes earlier. It was time to go. Surely, the kidnapper had phoned, and Bastian would have an update on that situation. But if the police didn't have Mercer and his team under surveillance, that meant only one thing—the kidnapper was tracking their movements.

"Learn anything useful?" Donovan whispered as they exited into the hot afternoon sun.

"The hospital uses some wicked good drugs. If I get a chance, I'll see if Veronica can slip me some." Hans smiled. "Might cure that headache of yours."

"So nothing?" Mercer asked.

"I might have been having a conversation with a space cadet with the progress I made. He just kept prattling on about chaps with blue skin. From what I gather, the injured men are not working with the kidnapper. So if you're right about an inside man, he's being questioned by the bobbies as we speak. Shall I pop over and see what I can discover?"

"No." Unlocking the car doors, Mercer got behind the wheel. "For once, we will go through official channels to get the necessary intel. No cutting corners."

"Did you get conked on the head too?" Hans asked.

Mercer didn't bother with a response. Their priority was recovering the Blaine family, and to do that, they needed to determine who engineered the abduction.

Arriving at their destination, Mercer walked at a fast clip to the flat. His senses were on high alert, scanning for the slightest hint that someone had been here. Finding nothing amiss, he opened the door to see Bastian being harangued by someone on the phone.

"You have to make this happen. Just bloody do it already. We don't have time to waste." Bastian pressed the disconnect button as forcefully as someone would slam down a landline. "Tell me you have something that will turn this mess around."

"What did the kidnapper say?" Mercer asked.

"Five million Euros are to be placed inside a bright blue duffel bag and left on Blaine's private pier at oh six hundred tomorrow." Bastian bit down on a pen cap, chewing methodically while he spoke. "He hung up before I could ask for more time. He didn't discuss the condition of the hostages. He didn't discuss anything. Just the amount, how it should be left, and where. What are we going to do?"

"Did the insurance come through? What about the trace? We need a location, an identity, a way to put things right."

"The insurance was approved, but it cost us our souls and autonomy on our next few cases. And we're still short." Bas rubbed his eyes, swiveling toward the computer monitor. "Like this bastard said, it's an untraceable SAT phone. They could be anywhere on the planet by now. Bring me something to analyze, and I'll work some magic. But given the givens, I'd wager it'll be another dead end."

"We have even less than before." Donovan dropped onto the couch. "The paparazzo impersonator disappeared around the same time some tosser knocked me out. Our hotel room's been compromised. We can't return. By now, the police must be crawling all over the building. At least, I imagine that's the response a shotgun blast and a body would have."

"Jules?" Bastian asked.

"It's of no consequence at the present." Mercer leaned against the wall, willing his mind to clear, but thoughts kept entering and distracting him. "We have no assurances and no reason to believe once the ransom is paid the kidnapper will release the Blaines. Why would we comply?"

"Because they aren't giving us a bloody choice," Hans said.

"We don't work like this. We don't negotiate with terrorists." An amused smirk crossed Mercer's face. That line, coined by the Americans and used by most of the Western world, had always entertained him, partly for the obvious lie and partly because non-negotiations meant tactical resolutions. That was something he could plan for and control.

"What are you thinking?" Worry etched Bastian's already stressed features.

"First, we need to determine who has the senator and his family. Second, we need to figure out who's targeting us. Third, we go back to the original plan."

"Which is?" Hans asked.

"We break the package apart and buy off the pieces. If we can get one hostage free with the insurance payout, we'll be able to formulate a plan, determine their location, and man a rescue." Mercer picked up the phone. "I'll make the call and renegotiate the exchange. The kidnapper ought to realize without assurances, he won't get a dime. Once that's done, we'll be on a clock. Prepare accordingly."

It wasn't a great plan, but they couldn't let some tosser lead them around by the short and curlies. They were negotiators. They were used to being in a position of control or at least one of equal footing.

A stray thought crossed Bastian's mind. He picked up the flip phone they recovered from Blaine's estate and scanned the recent call log, finding several calls to the local police. Based on the call duration, they must have gone unanswered or a connection was never established. Scrolling farther back provided a list of calls and texts of an otherwise personal nature. The device held nothing overtly sinister. It was yet another fruitless endeavor.

"Hans," Bastian tossed the phone to him, "grab that laptop and run a few reverse number lookups. I'm guessing this belonged to one of Blaine's staff."

Hans pressed a few keys on the phone while typing in numbers. "It must have been used to call for help. And we arrived too late."

Mercer slammed his palm against the wall, annoyed the kidnapper wasn't answering. "Bas, was the last call from the same number?"

"Yes." A new thought crossed Bastian's mind, and he turned back to the computer.

Four rings later, Mercer hung up. "He wants to keep the line of communication closed. He wants to make sure we can't renegotiate."

"We're dealing with one of our own," Bastian surmised. "He knows the playbook. The rules. The techniques. He's either a professional kidnapper or a

K&R specialist. Guaranteed he'll ring back in a minute or two. He wants to keep us off kilter."

"Then we throw the rulebook out the window. He didn't want the authorities involved, so we'll start there."

As predicted, a minute later, the phone rang, and Mercer stared at it.

"Are you going to answer that?" Bastian asked. "It would still be helpful to free at least one of the hostages, if nothing else."

Grabbing the receiver on the fifth and likely final ring, Mercer answered with a risky greeting. "When I call, I expect you to answer. If you refuse, I will not provide payment. Is that understood?"

"You are not in charge," the kidnapper said.

"Then who is? I want a name."

The man on the other end hesitated briefly. "John Wolf."

"Is that you, or the man whose cock you're sucking?"

"I am John Wolf, and you will address me with respect."

"Well, Mr. Wolf, let's talk about what's going to happen at six a.m." Mercer scribbled the name on a sheet of paper and handed it to Bastian. "You have provided zero assurances you will deliver as promised. Therefore, I cannot authorize the drop. You've acted violently, injured and killed hostages, and continue to rebuke attempts at compromise. I'm offering to trade one third of the ransom for one of the Blaines."

"Which one?"

"The boy."

"You will leave the money as directed, and once it has been picked up, you will receive instructions on where to find the hostage. Should you attempt to follow or place trackers with the cash, I will kill the senator. Is that understood?"

"Yes."

"Very good. And Mr. Mercer, don't confuse my generosity with weakness. This situation allows me and me alone to determine their fates."

The line went dead, and Mercer took a step back. "Bas, where's that magic you promised?"

"John Wolf, private military contractor, worked his way across the Middle East, performing clandestine negotiations to have POWs and the bodies of fallen soldiers released. Nearly a year ago, Darkfire, the private contractor, downsized. Wolf stopped working as a PMC and opened his own firm, training private negotiators. That tanked a couple of months later, taking with it most of his savings. After that, he fell off the radar. No job. He lost his house and wife. They divorced four months ago, and he has an open arrest warrant in the state of California from three and a half months ago for aggravated assault. No current address, no active credit cards, no financial activity of any sort. He dropped off the grid and became a ghost."

Mercer let the information seep in.

"Since we haven't seen the kidnapper, it's possible we aren't dealing with the same man. It could be one of Wolf's negotiator trainees or any of the thousands of John Wolves...Wolfs...in the world. This is just my best guess," Bastian said.

"Sounds pretty bloody promising to me." Hans looked at Mercer. "Shall I head to the police station now and see how the coppers are faring?"

"What about the body in our hotel room?" Donovan asked. "We ought to steer clear of the police."

"Unfortunately, we need access to the released hostages." Bastian exchanged a look with Mercer. "Anything on the body that ties us to the murder, aside from him being inside our hotel room?"

"Not that I'm aware."

"The suite wasn't in our names, but it doesn't take much to link us to the insurance company that rented the room," Bastian said.

"Hans, take Donovan with you." Mercer needed the intel, despite the risk.

"Good idea. If someone tries to knock us out, I'll get a good look at them while they're bonking Donnie on the head," Hans said, earning a searing gaze from Donovan.

"Identify any remaining threats, and do whatever is necessary to determine where the Blaines might be kept. Do not split up. We stay together, and we stay alive," Mercer said.

"What if I have to take a piss?" Hans asked. "Should I ask him to hold it for me?"

"Go," Bastian said before Mercer lost his patience. "Stay on comms. Transmissions every fifteen minutes, understand?"

"Yes, sir." Hans snapped to attention and saluted.

"I assume this is my punishment for being caught unaware. Trust me, I'll never let it happen again." Donovan patted the commander on the shoulder. "Thanks for the recovery, sir. Now let's get these bastards and go home."

EIGHT

After flipping through the employee dossiers, Julian rubbed his eyes and blinked away the grit. His concentration was shot. Concern over sending Hans and Donovan into the police station remained in his forethoughts, particularly since he'd need them to provide tactical support and couldn't risk the police detaining them.

"Did you have time to study the body?" Bastian's eyes remained on the screen in front of him.

"At least four gunshot wounds from a rifle. No blood. He exsanguinated elsewhere."

"And you're certain it's Blaine's security guard?"

"Yes."

"He might have been killed during the initial invasion. Any indication how long he's been dead?"

"Why does it matter?"

"We might need alibis. Having a TOD would make that easier."

"We didn't kill him. Wolf did." After several long minutes of utter silence, his mind latched onto something Bastian had said earlier. "Who did he assault?"

"Who?" Bastian asked.

"Wolf."

"A building security guard. The police report was vague. Give me a minute to find the name."

"Not necessary." Mercer studied the kidnapper's photo ID. "Assuming we have the right man, he's shown familiarity with tactics. He knows how to acquire and utilize actionable intel, and he has a team. When we determine his location, we'll have to plan accordingly."

"Jules, he's a killer who went so far as to take one of his government's own officials. We should be focused on the why."

"Isn't it apparent?"

"Enlighten me."

"The payoff."

"I don't believe that's it. His motivation is driven by something else. He has an unstable past. He was private military, which implies he has some sort of affliction that kept him from joining the regular military. He left that job and started his own business, but it flopped. His wife left. He assaults someone, flees the scene, and ends up in the tropics, kidnapping a senator. There's more to this story."

"Not every event in a person's life is connected. There is no cosmic plan. It's all meaningless."

"It matters, Jules. It all matters. In this instance, it might be everything. Wolf planned this out. He selected Blaine for a reason. You need to contact the senator's assistant and see if Blaine had any previous encounters with Wolf while I run an analysis on Darkfire. The private military group must have canned him for a reason."

"Why are we doing this?"

Understanding flooded Bastian after one look at

Mercer. "This matters. I know you don't want innocent people to be tormented the way you are. Plus, I'd like to even the scales by doing some good. We've done a lot of questionable things. It's best that we remove the question, don't you think?"

"We were following orders."

"I know, and it needed to be done. So does this." Bastian nudged Blaine's file closer. "The sooner we get this politician and his family home, the sooner we can focus on that new information you have regarding Michelle. I promise we will find her justice, but that's a marathon, and this, my friend, is a sprint. Quick pace." He clapped his hands together in rapid succession.

Reluctantly, Mercer picked up the phone and dialed Blaine's office. He had spoken to Teresa, Blaine's assistant, a few times already. After enduring a few moments of polite conversation, Mercer dove into the heart of the matter.

Sen. Blaine had received several threats regarding his stance against the use of PMCs. While being former military himself and in favor of most military action, Blaine had gone on record saying he wanted government troops to clean up the mess, not private citizens with M16s. Hiring contractors was doing nothing more than privatizing the military, decreasing jobs, and doing a disservice to the men and women in uniform. Blaine's changed stance had angered several of his constituents and congressional cohorts, particularly since he had served on the committee responsible for providing Darkfire the government contract in the first place.

"The politics are not important. What does this have to do with Wolf?" Mercer asked.

"John Wolf was one of the most vocal protestors. He'd been let go from his job when Darkfire's contract wasn't renewed. Understandably, he was angry. Many of our staff answered calls from Mr. Wolf and recommended employment agencies to him, but Wolf vehemently insisted this was the senator's fault. He had to be removed from several campaign functions for heckling. After that, he sent numerous, sharply worded letters to the senator. It got so bad Blaine filed a restraining order to keep the lunatic away from him," Teresa said.

"Did Wolf ever get violent?"

"Not that I'm aware."

"Was he stalking Blaine?"

"I don't believe so."

"Harassing him?"

"Mr. Mercer, did you not hear me say that he made several calls, sent numerous letters, and was thrown out for heckling? I'd call that harassment."

"Did he ever threaten to kidnap the senator or harm his family?"

"Oh." Teresa went silent. "I can check."

"Do that." Hanging up, Mercer rubbed his temples. He felt the coming onslaught of a wicked headache forming behind his eyes. "Incompetent pillock. Blaine received several threats, but no one paid them any heed."

"To be fair, they were mentioned briefly." Bastian could see playing devil's advocate was a pointless endeavor and dropped the argument. "Most of Darkfire's mercenaries were given the boot after the senator swayed enough of his fellow politicians to refuse to negotiate a new contract. Wolf wasn't the only PMC who became unemployed. Two thousand people lost their jobs."

"Brilliant. So if the tosser who abducted Blaine and his family isn't John Wolf, then we have another two thousand possibilities to explore."

"Let's focus on Wolf for now. Darkfire is a large contractor with several divisions and specialized operatives. Most of their employees could have easily transitioned into civilian life. Their skills could be used on other fronts. Private security, corporate security, policing, espionage."

"Wet work. Kidnappings."

"The point is Wolf must have other incentives to conduct a kidnapping."

"Blaine fucked with Wolf's lifestyle and livelihood. That's worthy of revenge," Mercer said. "This posh, blowhard bureaucrat passed a decree that destroyed the livelihood for thousands. Perhaps Blaine's getting what he deserves."

"What about the murdered guard or Barbara and Nathaniel? Is this what they deserve? Shall I ring Hans and Donovan and tell them to stand down?"

Mercer didn't speak. Something had caught his attention.

Bastian let out an agitated grunt. "Jules, I don't know what your issue is, but we can handle this without you. Maybe you should sit this one out."

Ripping a photo off the wall, Mercer held it out. "We know him." Their intel was wrong. The satellite images, the maps, the blueprints, the photos of Blaine's staff, it was all wrong. Mercer cleared the area except for three photos—Blaine, his wife, and his son.

"Are you daft?" Bastian stared in horror as Mercer undid hours of hard work by sifting through the intel and tossing dossiers and files to the floor while he searched for something of use. "Commander, stop."

Finding an obscure file buried beneath a pile of personnel records, criminal histories, and security system schematics, Mercer calmed. "You're right. He does know us."

"What the bloody hell are you dithering on about?"

"You said it earlier, Bas, but I didn't listen."

"Said what?"

"The kidnapper knows us." Mercer pointed to the image. "Take a good look at this man. I didn't recognize him until now. He's aged and cleaned up, but we've dealt with him before."

After several long moments, Bas took a step back, as if the photo were a venomous cobra. "Are you positive? He looks rather different now."

"It's him." Mercer covered the man's hair with his thumb and made some random pencil marks over his chin and cheeks. "Cover him in grime and give him a month's growth of beard."

"The Butcher of Belarus."

"I want to know every bloody thing about this bastard." Picking up the radio, he spoke to Hans. "I've identified one of the men working with the kidnapper. His current alias is Theodore Lamb, Blaine's accountant. Notify the police they are holding a very dangerous fellow."

"Right-o," Hans replied.

"Use caution. We've encountered Lamb before."

"Where?"

"The forests of Belarus."

"Bloody hell."

NINE

"It's a safe bet to assume Theodore Lamb isn't his real name." Since Mercer's revelation, Bastian had been scouring government databases. So far, it appeared this man's true identity was one of the best-kept secrets on the planet. "Oddly enough, this might be our most valuable piece of intel." Bastian clicked an image of six men wearing fatigues, war paint, and touting heavy artillery. "The man to the left of center is John Wolf. On the end is the Butcher. I've yet to get identities for the other four."

"They orchestrated the hostage situation and the kidnapping. The others must be the guards Hans saw through the fiber optic cable."

"What is a team of black ops doing with a senator and his family?" Bas gnawed on his thumbnail, giving the empty bag of licorice a dirty look. "Do you think they remember us? We weren't exactly enemies."

"We weren't allies either." Mercer went into the kitchen and returned with a bag of crisps. "Before you chew off your hand," he tossed the bag to Bastian, "you need to get that oral fixation under control, mate."

"I would if I could have a bloody cigarette or if our job wasn't so ridiculous." Bastian took a handful of crisps and crunched down, visibly relaxing. "Do you remember what their mission was in Belarus?"

"The same as ours. Infiltrate the enemy camp, gain intel on terrorist strongholds, and escape undetected."

"That last part wasn't in their mission briefing."

"Apparently not." Mercer and his team had arrived after the black ops mercenaries. The supposed enemy camp was littered with bodies. So much carnage and for nothing. By killing off a single terrorist cell, which was only a tiny part of a larger organization, the intel gathered was compromised, and the enemy retaliated in a major way, turning several neutral zones hot. "I thought that wanker was going to lob off your head."

"He did seem to fancy the idea until Donovan put one through his shoulder," Bastian remarked, recalling the grisly event.

"I would have put one through his skull. I should have. It would have saved me from doing it this time around." Mercer committed everyone's face to memory. "This is the team responsible. They spoke to us on the phone. They know we're on the other side of this. We must proceed with caution. At least one of them is operating on the island, watching us, assaulting Donovan, and planting corpses in our hotel."

"We know Lamb is on the island. Last we heard, he was in police custody. I don't imagine he'll stay there very long, but at least he's no longer with the family. That does increase their chances of survival. It also explains why the rescued hostages were in fear for their lives and wouldn't speak to us. He's a dangerous man. He's unstable and sadistic."

"He's not the only one."

"Jules, don't compete."

"Afraid I'll win?"

"Let Hans deal with that. He and Donovan are more than capable." Bastian keyed something in, but whatever he was hoping to find wasn't on the computer. "Two of them are on the island. Lamb is in custody, which means one of Wolf's other men must be near. The unknown was inside our hotel room." He tapped a few more keys frantically. "The security cams were wiped. I can't access any hotel footage prior to your arrival."

"What about the lobby?"

"Nothing. The entire system was erased." Bastian cast an annoyed look at the adjacent computer screen. "Looks like they pulled the same trick at Blaine's estate. I have yet to pull any data off the security hard drives you retrieved." He rubbed his palms against his trouser legs and started over.

"A man was waiting in the lobby around the same time I arrived." Mercer couldn't be certain if he was one of the men in the photograph with Wolf. "Lamb was just as close as you are now, and I didn't recognize him for who he really was. I should have."

"We didn't know about Wolf or his pack." Bas snorted, amused by the play on words. "You recognized him for what he appeared to be—Blaine's accountant."

"I will not make that mistake again. Once the police release him, we will take control and get answers. But for now, we have to find the wild card and even the playing field. They launched an attack against us, so we retaliate with a counterstrike."

"We don't have time. Hans and Donovan will maintain eyes on Lamb, but in less than twelve hours, we have to make the drop. If you want a feasible way to track the money, I need to focus on that. Make a decision. Wolf's team or following the ransom?"

As if to further complicate matters, the phone rang. Cursing, Mercer grabbed it, relieved it wasn't Wolf calling with more demands. Instead, Teresa had scanned in the most threatening letters and was in the process of e-mailing them to Bastian.

"I've already passed this along to the local authorities," she said. "They received copies when the letters first arrived. Do you want the officer's name who assisted in filing the report?"

"Do as you please." Hanging up without so much as a goodbye, Mercer took a steadying breath. "Focus on finding Wolf's team. I will handle the money drop myself."

"I don't like the sound of that," Bastian said.

The hours dwindled. The kidnapper wanted payment in European currency. That would require a few extra steps. So bearing the burden of another horrid phone conversation, Mercer rang the insurance company and requested the money be delivered per the usual armed guard to the senator's estate in six hours. Normally, he would have requested delivery at the hotel, but it was compromised. Everything about this negotiation seemed to be. Now he just needed to find a blue duffel bag and come up with a method of tracking it once it was picked up.

Mercer tore through their equipment, hoping to find something of use. Aside from the normal tools of the trade, there was nothing to aid in tracking the money. He sifted through the various dyes and markers, but they would be easily detected. Since he was dealing with a team of mercenaries, they'd be familiar with these tactics. Hell, they'd be expecting them, and Wolf made it clear there were to be no trackers and no one else at the drop.

Why the insistence on a blue bag? Mercer wondered, reorganizing his gear out of habit. The color would stick out on the private dock like a homing beacon. Sure, the estate was private and theoretically secure, assuming the police didn't decide to muck about, but any one of those island hopper tours or recreationalists on the water would spot it. All it would take was one curious individual for the money to disappear.

Wolf's intention was to attract distractions. The lack of sleep and frustration was slowing Mercer's mind. Giving the clock a glance, he climbed onto the bed. It was imperative he rest while he could. He could sleep for the next four hours and still have plenty of time to rendezvous with the deliveryman. After that, he'd use the cover of night to scout the waters surrounding the estate and hope to find some way of tracking the watercraft that would inevitably pick up the duffel.

With any luck, Wolf would use the same boat to drop off the boy, giving them the opportunity to plan a rescue. But for now, he needed sleep. Unfortunately, the only thing on his mind was going to the police station and showing the incompetent bobbies precisely how to conduct a proper interrogation, waterboarding optional.

Thoughts of violence and torture techniques weaved their way through Mercer's mind until he fell into a restless sleep. Before the usual nightmare could get worse, a slamming door roused him from his nap. Sitting up, he checked to make sure his hands weren't shaking before running a hand through his short hair and going into the main room. Hans and Donovan were back.

"Where's Lamb?" Mercer asked.

"We couldn't get close to him. The police refused to

release any of the rescued victims, and now the consulate's involved," Donovan said.

"How?"

"One of the lot had the wherewithal of phoning for assistance. I'm guessing it was the Butcher, hoping to keep us off him. Coward," Hans muttered.

"From the sounds of it, the whole group will be turned over to the U.S. government by daybreak," Donovan said.

"Did you fail to explain that Lamb is responsible for the kidnapping?" Mercer asked.

"Of course not, but the police don't care. They're happy to turn over the senator's staff and let someone else deal with these problems."

"First world problems." Hans smirked. "You should see this police station. The bobbies ought to be wearing swim trunks and Hawaiian shirts with the level of professionalism they practice. The captain is the only oddball in the bunch, and I'd say he's on the take. Whatever cartel or trafficker uses this island must pay him to look the other way, and so that's the official police motto when it comes to absolutely everything."

"We need to find a way to speak to Lamb." Mercer ran through the possibilities, settling somewhere between a stealthy jailbreak and a full out assault on the station. "You said they weren't being moved until morning. Are the victims detained, or are they free to move about?"

"We couldn't get close enough to see. We never made it past the detective's desk." Hans shrugged. "There's an entire back hallway, but I have no idea what's behind door number one, two, or three."

"I'll get some blueprints and a layout," Bastian volunteered, "but at some point, the police will connect the murdered security guard in our room to us. We need to limit our interactions with them. Busting out a prisoner won't do us any favors."

"So much for your plan to get the police involved," Donovan said. "It's probably for the best. After all, we're hardly prepared to deal with Wolf and his team, and we've dealt with them before. The police would be fish in a barrel. We don't need a rising death toll."

"Did you at least retrieve victim statements?" Mercer asked.

"They're rubbish." Hans held out a stack of photocopied documents. "Five men, assault gear, masks and hoods, they entered the house, forced everyone into one room. Later they separated the family from the workers. They roughed up a couple of the employees. One of them heard Mrs. Blaine screaming and Nathaniel crying. No one saw anything. The heat was blasting. The air was unbreathable. Some passed out. They were denied food and water, at least initially. At some point, one of the masked men opened fire and killed the security guard. Several others were hit, threatened, or shot. They spent two days being terrorized. They're in shock. There's nothing in these statements we don't already know or suspect."

"What about mentions of Lamb's involvement?" Bastian grabbed the pages and leafed through them.

"Not a word," Hans said.

"So at least two of these men are operating on the island. What are they doing?"

"Monitoring us," Mercer said. "Keeping us busy, framing us for crimes, screwing with the negotiation." He homed in on Donovan's side arm. "Have you checked your weapon?"

"It wasn't touched," Donovan said, but Bastian held out his hand for the gun. "I cleared the chamber and checked the magazine. Nothing's amiss."

"Let me have a looksy." Taking the gun, Bastian ejected the magazine and removed the sight and various parts. After a thorough examination, he retrieved an RF reader from his bag and waved it over the pieces. Then he reassembled the gun and handed it back to Donovan. "I wanted to make sure you weren't being tracked."

"Why the attempt at a frame-up?" Donovan asked.

"To confuse and delay." Something about the scenario struck a chord. "I'll be back later." Mercer stuck an earpiece in his ear. "If Wolf phones, patch him through."

"I thought we weren't supposed to go it alone," Bastian said.

The door to the flat slammed, and Bastian sighed. The commander wasn't particularly good at following orders, especially his own.

TEN

Waiting in the shadows near the guard station, Mercer couldn't imagine why anyone would holiday with a full staff. Didn't that defeat the purpose of getting away? No, the senator had come to the island for a reason. Mercer just wasn't quite sure what that reason was.

When an armored vehicle pulled to a stop, Mercer stepped out of the shadows. A guard got out of the vehicle with the briefcase. He came around to the front of the truck, maintaining a hand over his holstered weapon.

"Identification," the man said. Mercer pulled out his credentials and placed them on the hood. "Nice to meet you, Mr. Mercer. Where do you want the money?"

"I'll take it. Is that all of it?"

"Yes."

"In Euros?"

"Yes, sir."

Flipping the case open, Mercer leafed through the stacks of bills. Based on the heft and denominations inside, he assumed the count was accurate. He nodded curtly and removed a pen from his pocket, signing the custody form.

"Good luck, sir."

Mercer entered the guard station, watching the monitors for signs of movement while the truck pulled away. If Wolf's team was on the premises, they took extra care to avoid the cameras. However, Mercer didn't believe they were here. If anything, Wolf seemed determined to ensure the negotiation failed. This wasn't about taking prisoners or keeping hostages, at least not the unimportant ones.

Maneuvering around the laser grid and cameras, Mercer returned to the house. The senator and his family traveled privately to the island. They didn't go through diplomatic channels, request protection or special treatment from the consulate, and had no public appearances or charitable functions planned. This trip was meant to remain secret. Even the senator's supposed schedule prevented travel for the dates in question. Why did he come here? Why now?

Mercer removed an empty folder from inside the safe. On the tab was written *Trade Deal*. Whatever had been inside was gone now. Searching the room and the nearby office for a shredder, he finally happened upon the contraption, but there were no paper scraps inside. The trash bin was empty. Wolf must have taken it, or Blaine hid it somewhere.

Mercer tore through the rest of the office before returning to the bedroom. Emptying the contents of the dressers, drawers, and closets, he searched in and around every nook and cranny. He didn't waste time caring about the condition he left things. Someone of Blaine's status could afford to have the mess cleaned up, assuming Blaine and his family survived.

A passing glimpse into the boy's ransacked

bedroom caused Mercer to pause. Flashes of blood covering the kitchen floor shot through his mind. *Not now.* He desperately attempted to blink away the scene. His wife was choking, sputtering for air while he cradled her in his arms, promising her things he had no power to give. It should have been him. He deserved to die, not her. Not Michelle.

Gasping, he stumbled backward until he made contact with the wall, and he sunk to the floor. Acute anxiety was the term some doctor had given these episodes. The blinding headaches, the sudden dizziness, and the adrenaline-fueled shakes had made service under the Crown questionable. Of course, Mercer's recklessness, unstable demeanor, and disregard for the welfare of basically everyone had been the final nail in the coffin of his military career. This was his life now, working personal security and specializing in kidnapping recoveries, so he needed to pull it together. He had a job to do.

Slowing his frantic breaths, he counted to ten and climbed to his feet. Swallowing, he set his jaw and entered the bedroom. Something had triggered that unpleasant memory, and he was determined to figure out what it was.

As Hans noted earlier, the boy had put up a fight. Enough blood splattered the surfaces to indicate injury, probably a broken nose or a knocked out tooth, but not enough to indicate life-threatening trauma. That was the only positive thought that came to mind.

Nathaniel's room contained an assortment of toys, books, and games. The few shelves that remained undisturbed were orderly and well-maintained. No signs of dust or fingerprints littered any of the surfaces. The books looked new. Some of the games were still in the cellophane. Mercer scanned the titles. The collection was recent. Perhaps it had been purchased to keep the boy entertained during the holiday excursion.

The bloodied smears on the edge of the dresser made his blood boil. It was one thing to retaliate against an adult, particularly one who was responsible for costing thousands of people their jobs, but it was another to raise a hand to a child.

Mercer wasn't blind to the realities of the world or that children had been used as suicide bombers, soldiers, weapons, and human shields, but that was not the situation here. Nathaniel didn't ask for trouble. He couldn't control who his father was or what his father did. He was innocent.

Opening the top drawer, Mercer didn't know what he expected to find. Clothing filled the top drawers. The bottom drawer held a collection of blocks, constructed into various vehicles and characters. As he placed the creations on top of the dresser, a wheel fell off one of the cars, making a hollow thunk when it landed back in the drawer. The drawer contained a false bottom, but no matter how he tried to open it, the hidden compartment remained inaccessible.

He took a step back to assess the entire dresser for weaknesses and other hidden compartments. That was when a metal object, partially concealed beneath the dust ruffle, caught his eye. He lifted the thin metal blade off the floor. Instantly, he realized that's what his peripheral vision had picked up from the hallway and what had triggered his unfortunate memories.

The item wasn't a dagger or a typical weapon. It was a long, thin metal sheet about the width of a necktie. The end tapered into a curved hook. After inspecting the object but being unable to discern its purpose, Mercer placed it on the bed and continued examining the dresser.

He tipped it on its side for easier access to the

bottom. The furniture was constructed from several highly polished pieces of hardwood, but a narrow space existed between the bottom frame and the drawer in question.

Mercer knocked against it, following the hollow sound. At the back end was a slight depression and a tiny hole that would have been undetectable had he not moved the furniture. Removing the pen from his pocket, he used the tip to explore the hole, hoping it contained a hidden release for the drawer's false bottom. Scoffing at his own idiocy, he picked up the piece of metal and slid it into place. The tapered hook came to rest in the hole, and he gave it a tug.

The hidden bottom released with a pop. Dropping the dresser back to its feet, Mercer lifted the false bottom to reveal a folder. Inside were signed contracts, numbered accounts, proposals, and information on several illicit dealings. It didn't come as a surprise that Blaine had something to hide.

"Bloody fantastic." Mercer removed the documents, replaced the hidden bottom, and dropped the boy's blocks back inside. In the event Wolf's team checked the estate again, he wouldn't make it easy for them.

Taking the metal strip would further impede any attempts to gain access to the drawer and the hidden information that was no longer inside. Too bad he still had no idea if this was the reason behind the kidnapping. Right now, it was his best guess. Nothing else inside the home screamed motive.

The brisk walk back to the car caused the hairs on his neck to stand on end. He couldn't shake the feeling he was being watched. Informing his team of the possibility, Mercer promised to return to the flat after making one last stop. Should he not return, Bas could activate the SUV's tracker. The money was inside the boot, and one of them would have to make the delivery in the morning. Their only priority was getting the Blaines back alive.

ELEVEN

After circling the police station for twenty minutes, Mercer parked across the street from the main entrance. Night had fallen. A few palm trees waved in the breeze, casting eerie shadows across the front door. The streetlights on the island were few and far between. Two stood at either side of the police station's front entrance. Another one covered the rear lot and the service entrance.

Hans had spoken of a hallway that housed the victims, potential arrestees, and god knows what else. Adjusting the magnification on the binoculars, Mercer studied the lobby and main area of the police station from inside his car. Someone was manning the front desk. Another officer was seated in what was the entire station's bullpen, but the rest of the building appeared empty. A few darkened offices lined the rear wall, but like his men had said, there were no signs of the hostages or Lamb.

Getting out of the car, Mercer moved through the shadows. Still, he felt like he was being watched, but no other cars had driven by or parked. In the rear lot were three personal vehicles and four parked police cruisers. He pressed against the side of the building, watching for cameras while making his way to the rear door. He noted one security camera covering the entire back lot, but it wasn't pointed at the door.

He slid beneath the camera and pulled on the door handle. It didn't budge. He tried again, pressing down harder, but there was no give. At the side of the door was a keypad, but the numbers had faded away from weathering and age. After trying the simplest combination imaginable, a loud, angry buzz sounded.

He waited, hoping an officer would check on the cause of the disturbance and open the door. However, after a few minutes, he knew that wasn't going to happen.

He needed to find another way inside, and waltzing in the front door held no appeal.

Unfortunately the only other entry points led directly into the main lobby. He had no other choice. Returning to his car, he found the direct number for the police station and dialed. The man at the front desk answered, and Mercer watched him through the binoculars. Despite his many attempts to come up with a feasible excuse to lure the man away from his post, nothing worked.

"Forget it." Mercer disconnected.

When the officer left his desk to speak to the only other cop on duty, Mercer deciding now was his chance. He dashed across the street and up the front steps. As quietly as possible, he twisted the knob, hoping to sneak past the occupied officers and gain access to the back hallway without them noticing.

A chime sounded above his head. What kind of self-respecting police station placed a bell above the front door? The desk sergeant spun around, nodding a greeting to the recent arrival.

"May I help you, sir?"

"No." Mercer headed for the rear hallway.

"Sir, you can't go back there. Stop."

The other officer stood. "Sir, you were asked to stop." Unlike the desk sergeant, this copper drew his stun gun. "Freeze."

Writhing uncontrollably on the ground wasn't exactly how Mercer planned to spend his evening, and he didn't have the luxury of wasting time being tossed into a jail cell, even if it might be the best and fastest way of gaining access to Lamb. "I'm here to speak to the released hostages." He offered the least threatening smile he could muster and raised his hands. "I'm the Blaines' negotiator."

The officer squinted. "Yeah, maybe. You do look sort of familiar. Do you have any ID?"

"In my breast pocket."

"Get it out slowly."

Mercer nodded, hearing heavy breathing from the desk sergeant positioned behind him. Without having to look, he knew the other man also had his nonlethal weapon trained on him. Normally, he might risk it and attempt to subdue them, but they were freaked out and trigger happy. His chances weren't great in an enclosed space like this. Frankly, his chances would have been better if they had real firearms and not those stupid zappers. He could keep moving with lead in his arm, but not with fifty thousand volts disrupting his nervous system.

Producing his business card and ID, Mercer held them out to the side. The sergeant grabbed them. "He's okay," the sergeant said, and the officer lowered his weapon. "You should have checked in at the desk. I would have told you that you can't see the victims." He cocked a questioning eyebrow. "Didn't we just speak on the phone?"

"That's why I didn't waste my breath. My associates were here earlier. This is a matter of life and death. I need to speak to one of the released hostages."

"You can't."

"Why are you detaining them? Haven't they been through enough?"

"It's for their own protection. We needed to take their statements to build a case."

"The case is a kidnapping. You have no jurisdiction without the family's consent."

"Things don't work like that here." The officer nodded to the desk sergeant who lifted the phone and dialed a number. "All you need to know is the victims are safe."

"What have you done with them?" Mercer kept one eye on the man's hand, making sure he didn't reach for his weapon again.

"They are safe. The injured remain in doctor's care, and the rest are comfortable."

"I want to see them."

"They aren't here." The officer held his ground as Mercer inched closer.

Once he was within striking distance, Mercer grabbed the man's forearm with lightning speed. He kicked into his shin, dropping the officer to his knees. Mercer removed the stun gun, giving the officer a quick zap that flattened him to the ground. Without wasting time, he moved into the hallway.

It was a narrow, dingy thing. The first two doors had gold plaques. At the end was a thick metal door. Beyond that point were interrogation rooms and holding cells. Given the exterior dimensions of the building, none of them could be particularly large. Twisting the knob yielded no results. Mercer gripped the handle harder. But it wouldn't budge.

"Bloody locks." He removed his weapon, prepared to fire.

"I should arrest you," a voice said from behind. "You assaulted one of my officers. And now you're doing what? Breaking into my police station?" Caho sighed dramatically. "I thought we promised to share intel and help each other. If you wanted something, you needn't do anything more than ask."

"I must speak to Theodore Lamb."

"Ah," Caho nodded as if everything suddenly made sense, "I'm sorry I can't help you."

"Do not jerk me around."

"No, you see, Lamb and the rest of Blaine's staff were shuttled to the consulate an hour ago. We have no right to hold American citizens. It's best they get home quickly and safely."

"You're working with them."

"The U.S. consulate?" Caho asked, full of mock innocence. "But of course. Tourism is our primary source of capital. It's best to maintain good relations with powerful countries. Wouldn't you agree? Isn't that how a mercenary like yourself travels the world freely?"

"I am no mercenary. Where are the Blaines?"

"I assure you, I do not know. Is this an official request for police assistance?"

Mercer's glare spoke volumes.

"In that case, get out of my police station unless you want to see precisely how we deal with violent offenders." His cold gaze challenged Mercer. "We are aware of the homicide that occurred in your hotel room and now the assault on my officer. I have plenty to throw you and your associates in jail, and no one will see or hear from you for years. Trust me, our prisons will make you wish you were dead." He smiled. "Without you, the Blaines won't survive. You really ought to run along now." He stepped aside, gesturing to the open end of the hallway.

It took every ounce of self-restraint and the constant nagging of Bastian's voice in Mercer's mind to keep him from laying out Caho. As he walked past the snake, the only thought he could muster was that he had been right all along. The police captain was corrupt. There was no other reason why anyone in law enforcement would detain victims and shuttle them away as soon as the K&R specialists arrived. However, there were bigger fish to fry.

Without knowing the whereabouts of the victims and the Butcher of Belarus, Mercer left the police station. Time was running out, and he had another stop to make.

TWELVE

The island nightlife was coming into full swing. Parking on the side of the road next to a bright neon sign, Mercer observed a few kids attempting to sneak inside a club and called to them. Two ran off, but one stayed. Removing twenty dollars from his pocket, he smiled at the boy.

"Do me a favor?"

The boy stared expectantly at the cash. "What do you want, mister?"

"Let me know if someone approaches my car."

"Okay." The kid held out his hand for the cash, an amused smile on his face.

Ripping the bill in half, Mercer gave the kid one of the torn pieces. "When I return, you'll tell me and get the other half. Understand?"

"Yep." The kid took a seat at an outdoor table, close enough to the club to hear the music but still within visual range of the car. "What do you want me to do if someone shows up?"

"Yell fire."

Without waiting for additional questions, Mercer

inserted himself into the throng of people and searched for a place to buy a duffel bag. A few of the shops remained open. He ducked inside one of them. The store he selected was nearly empty. The clerk was unpacking boxes in the rear hallway.

A faint chime sounded from the back of the storage area. After a few moments, the clerk stopped what he was doing. He moved stiffly to a place behind the register and stared at Mercer with an intense fascination.

The clerk didn't appear threatening. If anything, he looked uneasy. A thin layer of perspiration erupted above his lip, and he busied himself with reorganizing the stack of brochures on the counter. Knowing to trust his instincts, Mercer went to the back of the shop and used the mirror from the sunglasses display to gain a clear view of the rest of the store.

The two other people inside the shop continued to browse, trying on hats and visors before making their selection. Once they left, the shop was empty, but from the way the clerk's eyes darted nervously to the storage room, Mercer knew something was wrong.

He moved toward the rear hallway. A man remained hidden in the shadows, visible only in silhouette. Perhaps he was a robber, but too many odd occurrences had happened already. Uncertain if the mystery man was one of the Wolf Pack, Mercer edged around a display to get a better look. But the angles were bad. If this man was part of Wolf's team, the others could be waiting outside.

Mercer reached into his jacket and removed his gun, keeping the weapon down at his side. He turned to the clerk and forced a friendly smile onto his face. "Do you have any more of these?" He picked up a souvenir bottle filled with sand.

"Tons. Check the next aisle."

Mercer ducked out of sight and crept along the back of the store until he ran out of cover positions. The scent of sunscreen and cologne filled his nostrils, and in that instant, he knew this was the man who had attacked Donovan.

Bursting from cover, he rushed the mercenary. The man turned, shifting into a defensive position. Mercer grabbed the man's wrist before he could fire. The mercenary dropped his gun, using both hands to grab the Sig from Mercer's hand. A shot went into the ceiling, dusting them with debris. The mercenary held tight, twisting and fusing his hands around the weapon to keep from being blasted.

Unable to pry the man free, Mercer elbowed him in the jaw and smashed the souvenir bottle against the man's forehead. The mercenary lost his grip on the gun and stumbled backward. Mercer launched a kick at his sternum. But the man parried, throwing up his arms in an X and pushing upward, knocking Mercer off balance.

Julian banged into the left wall of the narrow hallway, righting himself and firing at the man. The kidnapper ducked, retrieved his weapon, and fired blindly over his shoulder while he darted out the back. His shots went high and wide. Mercer focused his return fire, hitting the man near the inside of his shoulder blade. But that didn't stop the mercenary from escaping.

Amidst the sea of tourists, Wolf's teammate disappeared. Mercer gave the storekeeper a quick glance, making sure he hadn't become a senseless casualty, before pursuing.

Four restaurants were clustered around the rear exit, as well as several outdoor cafes and a live musical performance. The lack of adequate lighting made tracking the man next to impossible, so Mercer examined the ground for blood. But the trail disappeared just as suddenly as the man.

Mercer backed into the shop, grabbed a bright blue duffel from the front display window, dropped a hefty sum on the counter, and left. Handing the kid the other half of the torn bill, he gave the area a final look.

Before departing, he checked that the Euros and documents from the estate remained in the vehicle. If these wankers were smarter, they would have come up with a better plan than to stalk him and his team.

THIRTEEN

"That's why we aren't supposed to go it alone," Bastian chastised.

"I'm in charge."

"Pish." Bastian leaned back in his chair. "So what brilliant plan have you come up with for tracking the funds?" At Mercer's silence, Bastian snorted. "That's what I thought." He held out a tiny microchip. "Waterproof, low frequency, making it nearly undetectable to radio scans, but it requires close proximity. And I mean fucking close. A hundred meters, not much more. If it's submerged, the water will interfere. If it's shielded, the range drops dramatically. You'll get about thirty meters at best under those conditions."

"That's useless."

"This wasn't my priority, remember?" Bastian studied the duffel bag. "How many stores do you suppose sell this particular color? Maybe the point of the request was to cut our ranks. Are you sure it was the same man who attacked Donovan?"

"Positive."

"How do you know?"

"His horrid cologne."

"I don't imagine he had a splendid time in the forests. His dinner must have gotten one whiff of him and kept its distance." Bastian handed the photograph to Mercer. "Their actual identities are classified. Whoever joined the private military got their identities erased. These men don't exist anymore. Interpol and other crime databases are being searched, but I don't believe they had records prior to enlisting. DOT databases might be the only way to get actual identities, but for now, I say we stick with their last known aliases."

"We know Wolf and Lamb." Mercer pointed to the man he encountered inside the shop. "Who's this arsehole?"

"Damian Bear."

"And these other three shitheads?"

"Arnold Lemming, Sullivan Fox, and Carter Hawke. I won't waste time with their résumés. All we know for certain is they were private military black ops, and they've set their sights on Senator Blaine and his family. From the papers you brought back, it looks like revenge. Blaine made sure Darkfire's government contract was killed, so he could line his pockets with a kickback from another government contractor. Several, actually. These other companies were given more money once Darkfire was booted, so they each deposited substantial amounts in these numbered accounts. I assume the senator's anti-PMC stance was fueled by greed instead of any sense of loyalty to those in the service."

"Big surprise. Money always serves as an incentive."

"Be that as it may, Wolf wants more than cash."

"Revenge."

"No, Jules. Something else." Bastian spun one of the laptops around. "Sure, there were plenty of ledgers and account information hidden in the kid's drawer, but Lamb was hired to be Senator Blaine's personal accountant. If this is what the Wolf Pack wanted, Lamb could have gotten it an easier way."

"If it's not about cash, why request the exchange?"

"I have no bloody idea. Some of these papers don't make much sense." He pulled out a few sheets from between the folders. "I'd say they mean something, but I don't even know where to begin." He held up a sheet with half a dozen red points in what appeared to be a random order. "This isn't the only one." Bastian held out another page that had two sets of lines, one in black and one in blue. The lines made a path, but the paper was blank.

"Have you checked for invisible ink?"

"Fancy I retrieve my secret decoder ring from that box of cereal to help me out too?"

Mercer rolled his eyes. "Do what you can, Bas. Right now, we stick with the plan."

"Which is?"

"Prepare for the drop, track the money, and figure out some way to save the Blaines. Wolf believes he'll get the ransom. It should be enough to delay him from taking any brash actions."

"I don't know. Something doesn't feel right."

"None of it does." Mercer rubbed his eyes. In two hours, he'd leave to make the drop. "Have you been able to track Wolf's whereabouts or recent activity?"

"I'm sorry, Jules. When I said they don't exist, I meant it. They're ghosts. We know about the threats Wolf made. I've reviewed the letters and intel. There's nothing else to be gained from it. Four of the men aren't in any databases. No credit cards, no cell phones, nothing. Quite literally, I have a first and last name, and the rest is utter shite. None of it is accurate or even remotely believable. I've made some headway with Lamb because he was working for Blaine. I've compiled a dossier on his movements and whereabouts prior to the invasion, but it's smoke and mirrors. And now that he's been whisked away by the American consulate, I don't think we'll be able to touch him, let alone track his current position."

Mercer leafed through the information. "It tells us one thing."

"What's that?"

"They've been planning this for eight months."

"It's no bloody wonder we're behind. Honestly, we need a miracle. And I mean a real one, not the magic I work on a screen or by reading a mark."

"We'll work on it. Get some sleep. You haven't had more than a brief nap in the last three days. I'll need you lucid for what's to come."

"But I have to monitor the drop-off."

"No. Hans will accompany me, and Donovan can work the computers. Now go to bed, soldier."

"You bloody well better be in one piece when I wake up." Bas headed for the closest bedroom, looking over his shoulder and adding, "And you better be here."

Mercer found the mother hen routine amusing. Truthfully, Bastian was the glue that held the team together, and the glue that held the fragments of his sanity together. If it weren't for the analyst, the sorrow and rage would have taken hold a long time ago. Bodies would have piled up, and Mercer would be in prison or dead. Those weren't the best prospects, but outside the team and the mission, his only goal was revenge. After that, it didn't matter what happened to him. He died when Michelle did, but his body was too stubborn to accept it. Although it often made the threat of imminent death one of utter amusement rather than fear.

Taking the empty blue duffel, the microchip, and the case of cash, Mercer set up shop at the kitchen table. He removed the stacks of bills, placing them in even piles on the kitchen table. Then he went into the bathroom, found a sewing kit, and got to work stitching the microchip into the corner of the fabric where the excess piece of blue material hung loosely on the inside zipper.

"I could use a few centimeters taken in on my trousers." Donovan took a seat beside him.

"Maybe next time." When he was done, he cut the excess string and tossed the bag to the younger man. It was best to have a second set of eyes examine the handiwork for obvious tells. After getting Donovan's approval, Mercer refilled the bag. "You will monitor the estate's security system remotely. We will remain on comms."

"Are you sure you don't need a shooter?"

"Hans will do." Mercer scrutinized the bright blue. Something about the color clicked in his brain. "Blue skin." Without another word, he knocked on the bedroom door at the end of the hallway. "Hans?"

An annoyed grunt sounded, and Mercer let himself in.

"Lock door next time." Rolling over, Hans stared up at Julian. "What time is it?"

"We have an hour. What did you say about blue skin?"

"What?" Hans squinted, shaking himself as if he were having a bad dream. Kicking his legs over the side of the bed, he sat up and stretched. "The victim in the hospital said something about blue skinned blokes entering the house." He yawned and shook his head again. "It didn't make any sense. It makes about as much sense as you waking me up to ask about it."

"Get dressed. We leave in thirty."

"I thought you said we had an hour."

"What's wrong?" Donovan asked when Mercer returned to the kitchen.

"Divers. I need a map." Crossing to the stack of images, Mercer leafed through them but couldn't find anything that covered the underwater topography around the estate or private dock.

"I got conked on the head, so I'm gonna need a bit more than that, mate."

"They breached the estate via the water, but they didn't have a boat. They probably used scuba gear. I don't know if there are any underwater caves or alcoves close enough to use as a staging area or to surveil the residence."

"Like a reef or an underwater shelf. They'd need oxygen tanks or a rebreather, depending on how long they were staking out the estate. At night, it'd be even more difficult to see them in the water. They could sneak onto the grounds, and as long as they avoided the security system, they could bypass the guards. Once inside, they'd have leverage and hostages to complete the takeover."

"And they wore blue wetsuits," Hans said from the doorway. "I'm guessing that's why they want the money in a blue duffel bag. They plan on swimming away with it."

"It'll be daylight," Mercer pointed out. "They'll be easier to spot."

"Not necessarily. The water's murky. With the sun rising, there will be a wicked glare off the surface." Hans snorted. "I didn't realize we were dealing with seals."

"U.S. Navy?" Donovan asked.

"No, the ones that balance balls on their noses." Hans winked. "Have you seen these guys' names? Darkfire must literally be a zoo with hawks and foxes and bears, oh my."

If their assumptions were correct, the Wolf Pack, as Bastian dubbed them, would use one of their men as a diver to retrieve the ransom and swim back to the ship. Several underwater apparatuses existed that could make a long trek back to a boat easier. If they were using motorized equipment, the boat could be anchored far enough away to prevent detection from land but close enough for the diver to return in a timely fashion.

"How are you with a jet ski?" Mercer asked.

"I didn't realize we were on holiday. I can't say I have much experience, aside from a topless beach and a blonde pressed against me." Hans smiled. "But I got it to go pretty fast under those conditions."

"Bet she was disappointed," Donovan said.

"Enough." Mercer couldn't take this back and forth any longer. "Focus. We'll need to move quickly through the water to stay in range to track the ransom."

"A jet ski would be detected," Donovan said. "Anything with an engine will be seen or heard, especially if Wolf's team is in the water. We'd botch the exchange before it even occurred since he told you to come alone."

"I know." But there had to be another way. Mercer just didn't know what it was.

"I'll see what kind of satellite feed we can get of the surrounding sea and hope to track it from here," Donovan said.

"I can get a wetsuit and do some underwater exploration," Hans said.

"We don't have time," Mercer said. "We can't risk

compromising their retrieval. Get ready. I want you on overwatch. Maintain eyes on the estate with a clear line of sight to the dock and the surrounding area. Assuming they're water bound, having you close shouldn't hurt matters."

"Where will you be?"

"Inside the house."

"You're the boss." After selecting a long gun, scope, and wind gauge, Hans shoved a handful of ammo into his pocket and checked his side arm. A rifle and a handgun would help even the playing field should things go sideways, but taking out Wolf and his team at this juncture would be a death sentence for the kidnapped family. It was a double-edged sword. Without knowing where the family was being held, they would perish if anything happened to the kidnappers. "Ready when you are."

Nodding farewell to Donovan, Mercer hefted the bag. "Let's go."

FOURTEEN

Mercer placed the duffel on the dock, per the instructions, and looked out over the water. A few fishing boats were reeling in today's catch. Several yachts were moored nearby. Surprisingly, Blaine didn't own a yacht or boat, even though he had built a dock on the property.

Pushing his sunglasses against the bridge of his nose, Mercer scanned the surrounding area one final time. The bright sun had just breached the horizon, casting that annoying glare Hans had so eloquently pointed out. Even if the drop-off had been an hour earlier, they would still be operating blind.

Nightfall provided the best cover, but the vast majority of ransom exchanges occurred during daylight. That was one thing Mercer never understood. Perhaps it was because the funds were collected during the day or because it was easier to blend into the crowd and avoid detection when it wasn't atypical to be out and about. However, nothing about this kidnapping seemed typical.

He strode back to the estate and let himself inside. Upon arrival, he had deactivated the security system. This allowed for the possibility of an ambush, but he didn't believe Wolf would use this opportunity to plan another strike. The kidnapper wanted the five million. Attacking now would guarantee he never saw a dime beyond 1.6.

"In position," Hans' voice rang in Mercer's ear. "Everything's clear."

"Let me know if that changes."

Mercer's eyes remained fixed on the dock. From his current position, he was roughly a hundred meters from the drop point. At an all-out run, he could clear the distance and be on the kidnapper in fifteen seconds, or Hans could put the man down in the blink of an eye. The problem was tracking the bag once it was taken. For the first time, Mercer regretted not insisting on a face-to-face exchange, but Wolf was too smart to agree to that.

"Incoming," Hans said. "Two vehicles fast approaching the front entrance. Shall I intercept?"

"Negative."

"Sir?"

"Remain in position. Continue monitoring the area."

Mercer went to the front door. Two Land Rovers parked just beyond the gate, blocking the path that led back to the main road. From this distance, Mercer couldn't tell how many men were inside. The vehicles idled, their engines humming.

"What are they doing?" Hans asked.

"Waiting."

It was a trap. However, Mercer wasn't sure what Wolf had planned.

"Shit," Hans cursed.

"What?" Mercer aimed his weapon at the vehicles.

"The bag's gone. They took the money. I didn't see it happen. I missed it."

Before Mercer could reply, one of the vehicles gunned its engine, spitting gravel into the air as it reversed course. A moment later, the second followed. Its tires spun as it peeled out of the driveway and back to the main road. They were retreating.

The trucks had been nothing more than a distraction, and unfortunately, it worked. Their best chance to track the money vanished as quickly as the Land Rovers.

"How did you miss it?" Mercer asked.

"I don't know."

"That's not good enough."

"I swear no one made the pickup. The bag was there, and then it vanished."

"Donovan, anything from the tracker?" Mercer exited the back door with his gun in hand as he made his way to the dock.

"Nothing, sir. The house was beyond the tracker's transmission radius. Once you went inside, the transmission was lost."

"Bloody find it," Mercer said, more to himself than anyone else. He stepped to the edge of the pier, gazing into the depths of the crystal blue water. From this angle, he could see clearly, but looking into the distance sacrificed all visibility due to the sun's reflection on the water's surface. "Any satellites overhead?"

"Working on it," Donovan said.

"Hans, any idea which direction the vehicles were headed?"

"Southwest, toward the main marketplace."

"Brilliant. I'll attempt pursuit. Return to base camp."

"Sir," Donovan interrupted, "the kidnapper's

phoning."

"Bloody fantastic. Patch him through and run a trace."

"You can pick up the hostage at the central marketplace. You might want to hurry," Wolf said.

"We complied with your demands. I better find the package intact."

"You will, but depending on how quickly you get there, he might not be breathing." Wolf chuckled. "Like I said, hurry."

The line went dead, and Mercer sprinted to the car. "Donovan, any luck on that trace?"

"Negative. The call didn't last long enough."

Mercer sped down the road in the direction the Land Rovers had gone. If only he had done something to intervene when they were on the property, maybe this would be over now. Wolf's threat echoed in his mind, and Mercer couldn't shake the feeling he was unprepared for whatever he was about to find.

Five minutes later, he screeched to a stop. One of the vehicles was abandoned on the side of the road. It appeared to be unoccupied, but it could be another trap or distraction.

Mercer ran toward the truck. The driver's door was ajar, but no one was nearby. He dropped to a crouch, checking to see if the vehicle was wired, but he didn't see any explosives.

A glimpse through the opened car door revealed a body bag on the rear seat. Mercer threw open the door. The contents of the bag were far too large to be a child, and fearing he was about to reveal the body of Barbara Blaine, he gulped down some air and reached for the zipper. He grit his teeth, annoyed to find it locked in place.

Reluctantly, he tucked his handgun into his holster, needing both hands to unzip the bag. He found

Senator Harry Blaine inside. His skin was pale, his lips turning blue. A plastic bag was duct taped around his head with a small hose running into the bag. It was connected to an emergency oxygen tank. The tiny tank was intended for recreational divers and held roughly ten minutes of air. No more but possibly a lot less.

Ripping the bag to shreds, Mercer tore at the duct tape around Blaine's neck while he felt for a pulse. Tilting Blaine's head back, he checked the senator's airway and gave him mouth to mouth, hoping it wasn't too late. After a few breaths, the man gasped, and Mercer leaned back. "We've recovered the senator."

Blaine's eyes fluttered open, and he panicked, struggling to get away from Mercer. "Who the hell are you? Stay back. Stay away. Where are we? Where did you take me?"

"Sir, I'm here to help. Hold still." Mercer removed a knife from his belt, cutting the tape that bound the senator's arms and legs. "I'm Julian Mercer. I've been negotiating with the kidnappers on your behalf."

"My behalf?" Blaine choked. "Who are you?"

"A security specialist hired by your insurance company to ensure your safe return."

"What?"

Mercer refrained from answering the same question again. "Are you injured?"

"Am I injured? What the hell do you think?"

That I shouldn't have bothered removing the duct tape. "Sir," Mercer began, but Blaine silenced him.

"I want to speak to the police. I want an ambulance, and I want to know where my wife and son are. Did you find them? Are they okay?"

"What's the last thing you remember?" Mercer handed his phone to the senator. If the man wanted to speak to the police, he could call them himself.

"They took Barb and me and tied us up. We had to breathe through these hoses. It must have been some kind of torture. I don't know. I blacked out."

"They did the same thing to your wife?" Mercer practically snatched the phone out of the man's hand in order to get him to answer.

"Yes. I didn't see her after that."

"Fuck." Mercer stepped out of the vehicle, searching in all directions for the other Land Rover. "Someone get me a location on the second vehicle. Now. The wife might be inside."

He didn't spot the car and hoped Blaine was mistaken. The senator wasn't breathing when he arrived, and having to track a second car would take too long. She'd be dead, if she wasn't already.

Searching the front seat, he didn't find a GPS or map. Blaine had to be wrong. The man might be suffering from brain damage. Hopefully, he hallucinated and wasn't thinking straight. Mercer's mind traveled down dark paths, but none of them provided a solution that would save the woman, only options on what to do after they found her dead.

Blaine's annoyed nasally voice and the blaring sirens drew Mercer out of the front seat and back to the rear door. Blaine had pulled himself out of the car and leaned against it. He looked better upright than inside a body bag, but he wasn't in a trusting mood and kept his distance.

After making a final attempt to assist, Mercer stepped away, giving Blaine space. The man was in shock, having been moments away from death and subjected to god knows what for the last few days.

Several police cars and an ambulance surrounded the truck.

"Stay where you are," a cop bellowed, eyeing Mercer while the other officers questioned the senator and checked the vehicle.

There wasn't time for this nonsense. Barbara Blaine could be suffocating to death, and there was nothing Mercer could do about it. He listened to the chatter through his earpiece, but Donovan couldn't locate the second truck on any of the island's cameras. From the constant sound of car horns, Hans was taking several liberties with the traffic laws, but he hadn't spotted the vehicle either. The island was small, but the vehicle could be anywhere.

As the moments ticked by, Mercer became more anxious. He checked his watch. Time was up. If Mrs. Blaine had been in a similar state, she was dead now.

As the paramedics busied themselves with helping the senator, the police relaxed. Julian wanted to run, to search, to find Wolf and snap every bone in the man's body. But he couldn't. Not yet.

Crossing his arms over his chest, he attempted to silence his rage. Unfortunately, the shift in position made his side arm visible, and when the copper turned back around, he drew his weapon.

"Sir, don't move. Hands up."

"You wanker, don't you realize I rescued the senator? I had to breathe life back into his bloody body. Do you think I'd waste my time doing that if I was going to shoot him?" The words served as an outlet for the growing apprehension that had been building since discovering Barbara Blaine was likely dead or dying.

"Need an assist?" Hans asked. "I'm on my way. Don't start a firefight without me."

"No," Mercer said, "continue searching."

The officer removed the gun from inside Mercer's jacket. Holding it up, he sniffed the barrel and checked the magazine. But the weapon hadn't been fired, and there was no evidence on the senator or in the car to suggest otherwise.

"Call your bloody captain. We spoke yesterday," Mercer said.

Before the officer could say anything, another cop called for help. He was at the boot with the lid raised. Mercer watched as Barbara Blaine was pulled from inside. She was bound in the same fashion as her husband. Her lips were blue, and her skin was white. The officer laid her on the ground, cutting her free and pulling the bag off her head. He yelled for the paramedics who were checking the senator's vitals.

After pumping air into her lungs and starting chest compressions, they loaded her onto a stretcher. Blaine stumbled toward them. When he turned around, his eyes found Mercer's.

"Why didn't you help her?" Blaine screamed. "Didn't you say you were working on our behalf?"

"Sir, we need to go," the ambulance driver insisted.

One of the cops slammed the door shut, and the ambulance took off. A single police car followed.

The remaining officer narrowed his eyes at Mercer. "It appears we have more to talk about."

"I'm done talking." Mercer yanked his gun out of the man's hand and returned to his car, ignoring the shouted threats. Since the police didn't act last night, they sure as hell weren't going to do anything rash now.

FIFTEEN

Mercer was livid. Huffing like a bull preparing to charge, he ripped the phone from the cradle. He smashed down the buttons, dialing Wolf's number. Before the call connected, he slammed down the receiver. Phoning now would only endanger the boy. Letting out a yell, he threw the table across the room.

Donovan remained silent, watching as it crashed against the wall. Staying out of Mercer's way would be best until the commander calmed down. However, Mercer had passed the point of no return. He stormed into the kitchen and yanked the cabinet door open. He grabbed a glass, but it broke under the force of his grip. He reached for another one. Hurling it with all his might, he watched it shatter against the wall, unable to stop himself until the entire cabinet was empty.

Bastian stepped into the kitchen, eyeing the shards that covered the tile from the decimated tumblers. Without uttering a word, he opened the fridge, removed a container of juice, and drank from the carton. Replacing it on the shelf, he closed the fridge door, gauging his friend's level of control.

Mercer leaned over the sink, his shoulders rising and falling as if he'd just swum the English Channel in a single breath. "What's her status?" His hands shook from the sudden explosion that had overtaken his body, and he gripped the edge of the counter, watching bemusedly as blood dripped from his palm, through his fingers, and to the ground. He was numb. No physical pain could touch him right now. Hopefully, that would also apply to psychological anguish.

"Bleak," Bastian replied. "She hasn't regained consciousness. They don't know if she will."

Blaine's accusation ran on a loop through his mind. *Why didn't you help her?* Squeezing the bridge of his nose, Mercer fought to keep himself in check. His sanity was a precarious thing. His mind kept mixing images of Michelle's last moments with Barbara Blaine being pulled from the boot of the truck. It was a sadistic game of self-torture.

"Jules, they still have Nathaniel."

"I know." After washing away the glass and excess blood, he wrapped a towel around his hand and faced his friend. The cold, apathetic façade was back in place. "We need to speak to Blaine."

"Hans is with him now. Until the senator knows something definitive about his wife's condition, we can't expect him to focus on this. It's our show unless he says otherwise. Hans will keep us apprised."

"Brilliant."

A shrill electronic noise came from the other room, and Donovan appeared in the doorway. "Sorry to interrupt, but the kidnapper's calling." At the sight of the mess in front of him, he added, "I can answer, if you like."

"No," Mercer tossed a warning glance in Bastian's direction, seeing the protest forming on the other man's lips, "I will speak to him."

Moving into the command center, Mercer reached for the phone. The base had separated from the buttons, but it appeared functional. Lifting the handset, he waited for the kidnapper to speak. The sound of Wolf's voice grated on his every nerve ending, like nails across a chalkboard, but the security specialist held it together.

"Did you find Blaine?" Wolf asked.

"Yes."

"Was he intact?"

"The package was damaged. Any other dealings will require a face-to-face exchange. Those are the new terms."

"Tut tut. You either haven't spoken to your client, or he's unable to speak. Then again, maybe the little woman is the one not faring well. Oxygen deprivation is known to cause brain damage, paralysis, and death."

"Your point?" Mercer curled his fingers into a tight ball.

"Senator Blaine knows what I want. He will have you fetch it and bring it to me. If not, he'll never see his precious baby boy ever again. Not that he actually gives a flying fuck about his progeny, but the wifey certainly does. She wouldn't forgive him if anything happened to their son. Then again, it looks like she's not long for this world. It's a shame you didn't think to look in the cargo hold. Where else would a good soldier hide his valuables?"

"You shouldn't expect to get a thing from the family after what you've done."

"Oh, I will. Mark my words, Mercer, the Blaines will give me precisely what I'm after, or I'll use little

Nathaniel to chum the waters. Pass that along."

The line went dead, and Mercer placed the phone down. "Wolf has someone at the hospital. He's aware of Barbara's condition."

"I'll notify Hans." Donovan reached for the radio.

"What about demands? What about Nathaniel?" Bastian asked, concerned with the sudden calm that had overtaken Julian.

"Supposedly, Blaine is aware of Wolf's newest demands. The kidnapper is confident payment will be forthcoming."

"He must be, if he was willing to release his primary target and Barbara."

A bitter scowl played across Mercer's face. "The point of releasing the wife was to demonstrate his ruthlessness. Nothing more."

"Scare tactics." Bastian understood the implications. "The child will face something much worse if his father doesn't cooperate. Still, there must be an ulterior motive behind the senator's release. Do we have a timetable for when the next payment is expected?"

"No."

"What do you think Wolf wants?"

"To die slowly." Mercer unclenched his fist, pulling the soppy towel loose. "I should bandage this."

"Jules," Donovan piped up, "Blaine wants to speak to you in person as soon as possible."

"Are the police present?"

Donovan nodded.

"Is that a problem?" Bastian asked.

"Perhaps." Mercer rubbed his eyes. "No matter. I'll go."

"No." Donovan shifted his gaze to Bastian, then back to Mercer. "He wants to meet this evening. His wife's in a coma, so he'll be checking in to the closest hotel. Once he's settled, he expects to speak to you."

"Fine." Without waiting for his team to debate the merits of this decision or the possible implications, Mercer left the room.

* * *

Mercer didn't want to have another face-off with the island's gendarmes, but his client requested to meet in person. And since Blaine would be dictating the terms of the negotiation from here on out, that didn't leave Mercer much of a choice, particularly when Blaine possessed knowledge regarding Wolf's whereabouts and latest demands.

The hotel lobby contained two uniformed police officers, but that was the extent of their presence. They paid no heed to Mercer or Bastian as the men entered. The hotel manager phoned Blaine's room, passed word along, and directed the negotiators to the nearest elevator.

Mercer noted the lax security. No wonder Blaine had been targeted. The only way Wolf's job would have been easier was if the senator had a bull's eye tattooed between his eyes.

He knocked on the door. The shuffle of heavy footsteps sounded from the other side. Then the door opened an inch.

"Senator Blaine," Mercer said, his voice as stiff as his posture, "may we come in?"

The four gorillas clad in Armani suits appeared far more formidable than the island's police force, and Mercer reconsidered his previous assessment. Blaine pushed his way between the guards. He nodded to one of them, and the largest man stepped away from the door, allowing the specialists to enter. After sizing up the negotiators, the bodyguards returned to their positions. The senator wasn't willing to take any more chances. Too bad he hadn't been this cautious a few days sooner.

"Have you spoken to the police?" Mercer asked. "Will they be taking over the recovery?"

"Recovery?" Blaine scoffed. "You think these yokels could handle a man like PMC Wolf? You must be out of your fucking mind."

"He is," Bastian muttered under his breath.

"What?" Blaine snapped.

"Bastian Clarke." He extended his hand, but Blaine ignored the gesture. "We've been working tirelessly to compile intel on the kidnappers. Unfortunately, we have been unable to pin down their current location. Anything you can tell us will be of great use."

"Where the hell were you this morning?" Blaine asked. "Shouldn't you have been assisting with the recovery? If you had been there, you could have helped my wife. She wouldn't be where she is now if you'd been better prepared."

"Sir," Bastian began, diplomatic as always, "there were too many possibilities to explore."

"Silence." Mercer stepped between Bastian and Blaine. "Do not blame my men for this. The fault lies with me alone. We were hired to work on your behalf. However, our continued service is up to you."

"The hell it is. Wolf made it clear he will only speak to you. So what kind of beef does this asshole have with you?"

Mercer shrugged.

"We may have encountered him briefly during a military operation several years ago," Bastian volunteered. "He and his men didn't leave a lasting impression. Senator Blaine, this isn't about us. This is about you. This is about revenge or leverage. Do you know why Wolf targeted your family?"

Blaine's gaze dropped to the floor, and he shook his head.

"Rubbish," Mercer spat. "He knew you'd be here on holiday with your family. Your own accountant works for him. I imagine they want access to your numbered accounts."

If the senator was surprised by the revelation, he didn't show it. Instead, he took a breath. "Leave us." He waited for the bodyguards to file out of the room. "What else have you discovered?"

"Your voting record, mate," Bastian said.

"This isn't a guessing game," Mercer said. "Time is of the essence. We believe Wolf will kill your son should you not fulfill his demands."

Blaine rubbed his neck, picking up a photograph of his family. "Gentlemen, I'm between a rock and a hard place." He put the photo down, looking up with all the remorse and resentment of any elected official who had been caught in a scandal and was in the midst of denying the allegations. "The accounts can be drained, but Wolf wants a hell of a lot more than money. This isn't about dollars and cents. This is about something else. I don't have the power or authority to get him what he wants."

"Your wife might never wake up, and your son's life is in danger. Are you grasping the reality of this situation?" Mercer asked.

"Maybe Barbara wouldn't be where she is if you'd done your job," Blaine shot back.

"You're right, but I didn't put her in the boot of the truck with a bag over her head. Wolf did, and he will pay."

"Sir," Bastian interjected, "what does Wolf want?"

"Money, power, the little things in life. He wants back what was his. It's about what he believes I took away from him."

"What was that?" Mercer asked.

Blaine ran his tongue along his teeth, making a sucking sound to buy a few moments. "He wants his livelihood back."

Mercer gave Bastian a pointed look, as if to say *I told you so*. "Is that why he wants five million Euros?"

"Five million?" Blaine's eyes went wide. "Euros, not even American dollars. Shit, that's like...shit...what the hell is that? Eight million or something?"

"Or something," Bastian replied, curiously studying the man who seemed more upset by the amount than the fate of his son. "The money is tangible. Based on the accounts we discovered, it might wipe you out, but it's doable, yes?"

"Yes and no. Those accounts contain shared capital from a recent venture. Some of the money belongs to a business partner. We made a deal, but touching those accounts now would raise several red flags. Neither he nor I can afford that."

Mercer bit back the vile comment. "Then we'll have to meet Wolf's other demand. What is it?"

Blaine shook his head.

Taking a step closer, Mercer placed his palms on the desk and stared into the senator's eyes. "I spoke to Wolf earlier. He said you would have me fetch it for him. That sounds pretty tangible to me."

"We're here to help." Bastian hoped to counteract the menacing tone in Mercer's voice. "We've pulled off a miracle or two. We'll figure it out or find a way to stall for time."

"What I'm about to say does not bear repeating. If either of you utters a word of this to anyone, you won't live to see your next birthdays."

"Threats?" Mercer asked.

"No. I just want you to understand the gravitas of these circumstances." Blaine moved to the window and peered outside, as if drones might be homing in on his location. "The reason Darkfire's government contract was revoked and the PMCs recalled was to establish new lines of trade. Unbeknownst to me, withdrawing like that compromised a government-sanctioned operation in the Middle East, undermining missions and objectives of several of our defense and intelligence agencies, as well as our men on the ground."

"You turned over state's secrets to other entities," Mercer said.

"That's treason," Bastian said.

"Punishable by death," Blaine added.

SIXTEEN

Mercer scanned the room, eyeing Blaine's personal effects while Bastian attempted to pry additional information out of the senator. Giving Wolf what he wanted would trade one life for another. That wasn't precisely how negotiations were meant to go, unless the life being sacrificed belonged to the kidnapper. However, Nathaniel was just a boy. He was innocent. His father was another story.

"What kind of trade lines did you hope to establish?" Mercer asked.

"Illegal ones." Blaine's caginess wasn't helping the situation. "It doesn't matter. What matters is Wolf wants me to hand over everything on my associates and their business ventures."

"Wouldn't that set everything straight?" Bastian asked.

"No." Blaine fought against his own sense of self-preservation. "Darkfire isn't a government contractor anymore. I made sure of that. And even if they were, Wolf doesn't work for them. I'd simply be selling out my new partners."

"Like you sold out your country." Mercer didn't bother to mask the disdain from his voice.

"I didn't know that at the time. How was I supposed to know we were using contraband as a bartering chip to strengthen pro-American forces?" Blaine asked.

"That's how wars are won, mate." Bastian licked his lips. "World powers supply factions within a region with weapons and artillery to fight against insurgents or to garner support to overthrow unfriendly governments. Nine times out of ten, it backfires somewhere down the line, but that's neither here nor there."

"I don't think it's guns. Well, maybe." Blaine shook his head. "I don't really know what it is. I was approached by several private sector bigwigs. They wanted to expand their business reach, but they needed the government to back off a bit. They said they would support my campaign if I voted against the use of PMCs."

"You did more than that," Mercer said. "Did these bigwigs approach your colleagues as well?"

Blaine shrugged. "It's politics. The majority vote along party lines, so whatever stance the party has, they support. Only a handful of votes are actual swing votes. It's possible others were offered a similar deal, but no one told me about it. It's a secret."

"Did they tell you what business they were trying to expand?" Mercer asked, but Blaine looked away.

"They wanted control of the drug trade," Bastian surmised. "You partnered with drug lords. Are you daft?"

"They're businessmen. They sold me on the idea by saying it was like venture capital. I could see giant returns on a small investment."

"What investment?" Mercer asked.

"After the vote went through and Darkfire's contract expired, there was a sudden gap in our military presence. Privately funded security teams volunteered to move into the region and maintain the area until more troops could be sent over. I invested in these groups, and I've been receiving constant returns on my initial investment ever since."

"And that didn't seem sketchy to you?" Bastian raised an eyebrow.

"The money in those numbered accounts came from your investment?" Mercer asked, and Blaine nodded. "Fucking hell, you've been taking blood money from a cartel."

"It's just dividends on my investment. It's my cut." Blaine couldn't accept the reality of the situation, or perhaps he simply refused. "There's nothing illegal about that."

"Then there's nothing illegal about your vote either," Mercer said. "Pay the kidnapper and be done with it."

"The vote wasn't illegal," Blaine repeated.

"Then why did you say this compromised your government's agencies and operations?" Bastian asked, the wheels in his brain struggling for traction. "What else did you do?"

"I might have provided those private security groups with classified information concerning our presence in the region. The information exploited our weaknesses and divulged names and locations for several of our operations. I just...I didn't realize it at the time. I thought...y'know...it just looked like bases and strongholds."

"And you willingly turned it over?"

"I thought these temporary private security groups needed that info to maintain order. How would it have looked if the senator who voted against PMCs and then supported the use of temporary security groups allowed those men to be slaughtered?"

"Pretty shitty." Mercer glared at him. "But not nearly as bad as selling out your own government."

"I didn't."

"You did."

"No use denying it," Bastian said. "That's why you're afraid of this coming to light. It's what Wolf is counting on. He knows you have to control the fallout to weather the cover-up. Tell us what he wants."

"He wants everything I gave to my business associates. But I can't give it to him. I can't sell out my partner."

"You mean the cartel," Mercer corrected. "Have they threatened you?"

"Not in so many words. My partner has access to the accounts as a type of insurance policy to make sure I don't renege on our agreement or use the intel to turn him over to the authorities. He doesn't like it when things go wrong. That's why I had to come to this hellish paradise in the first place."

"What?" Mercer's brows arched in confusion.

"I received a communication from my partner requesting I meet him here in person. It was last minute, but it sounded serious."

"How so?" Bastian asked.

Blaine exhaled, annoyed he was being asked to explain himself, his dirty political dealings, and illegal activity. "Last week, some soldiers burned through the fields, destroyed the crop, and jeopardized everything."

"For you." Mercer looked at Bastian, seeing the comprehension dawn on his associate's face. Wolf had done the deed himself to lure Blaine and his partners into the open. "Did you meet with the drug lord?"

Blaine glared, seconds away from throwing a punch. Instead, he cleared his throat. "When I arrived, I contacted my associate, but he changed his mind. He never said why. He just said it might not be safe. The next thing I know, these whack jobs invaded my beach house, took my staff captive, and threatened my family."

"Who's your partner?" Mercer asked.

"We need to know," Bastian insisted. "Are you absolutely certain the cartel didn't hire Wolf to eliminate potential witnesses and save some green on those dividends?"

"If that were the case, I'd already be dead. My partner has the bank information. He wouldn't waste time asking for it. He would simply empty the accounts and kill us."

Mercer snorted, amused by the sudden reality check the senator was exhibiting. Apparently, he finally realized denial wasn't going to get his son back or get him out of this mess.

"Do you think we could convince him to meet?" Bastian asked.

"No. Our connection is secret. None of this is supposed to become public. This spectacle Wolf has made has the potential of becoming very public. The police already know. You know. My staff at home knows. This is already too big. The rest of the Senate will eventually hear about it. If an investigation is opened, the risk of exposure will ruin my career and possibly jeopardize my freedom or even my life."

"With all due respect," Bastian began, "you need to realize your son's life is an irreplaceable commodity, and he's in danger at this precise moment. Saving your reputation should be the least of your problems right now."

"That's not what I'm saying."

"Come on, Bas," Mercer said, "there are more practical things we should be doing. At least some of us are determined to save the boy."

"Mr. Mercer, that is not what I'm saying. I would give anything for Nathaniel. I would give anything for my wife to wake up. But you've already failed once. I don't want to give you more ammunition to fire against me. Frankly, I've already said too much. I told you everything. What are you going to do about it? How is this going to help Nathaniel? Are you just going to wait for the police to arrive to help again? Because they were a little too late, and so were you."

Mercer turned around. His fists clenched. Fortunately, he knew better than to act. The bodyguards would take such violence very seriously. "You said you'd give anything. We need the money or the intel. I'm bloody sure Wolf will demand both before this is over. Either you pull it out of your tight arse, or you give us everything you can and hope we can mount a tactical rescue. If Wolf isn't appeased or we're not successful, your son will die quite horrifically."

"Let's start with where you were taken, and we'll go from there." Bastian glanced at Mercer. "You might want to brew a pot of tea, mate. We'll be here a while."

SEVENTEEN

"Bas, get to the bottom of those accounts. If we need to approach this drug lord, we will." As soon as they left Blaine, Mercer began barking orders. However, he had yet to address the elephant in the room, and Bastian feared what would happen when he did.

"Have you gone mad? Aren't there enough people gunning for us?"

"With Blaine's limited cooperation, we may have no other choice." Mercer gazed out the window, watching the palm trees pass as they drove back to the flat. "This unnamed associate potentially lured Blaine here. He could be behind the attack, or he wants to end Wolf, just like we do."

"I hate uncertainty." Bastian caught Mercer's eye before returning his focus to the road. "There's one thing I don't understand. How did Wolf know enough about the senator's dirty dealings to orchestrate this type of planned operation? It's been in the works for months now."

"The vote. It wouldn't have taken long to trace the stench back to that political pile of shit. After that,

Wolf must have created Lamb's persona and credentials, came up with a convenient reason to replace Blaine's previous accountant, and planned from there."

Bastian tapped his fingers against the steering wheel. "After all this, we still have no way of determining where Nathaniel is being held. This is bloody insane. Did you gather anything from Blaine's description of where they were held after Wolf took them from the estate?"

Mercer shook his head. "He did a fair job describing the lower cabin of the speedboat, but the rest didn't make sense. I believe Blaine is lying."

"That's possible. But why? He disclosed his illegal activities. Why would he deceive us about the kidnapper's location?"

Wolf's words echoed in his head. The kidnapper didn't believe Blaine would do anything to save the child. "Are we certain Nathaniel is Blaine's son?"

"You're shitting me." Bastian gave Mercer an incredulous look. "We would have uncovered a record of it when we compiled our dossiers. There's no look of impropriety. No extramarital relationships by either of the Blaines."

"Maybe it was left out of the papers." Appearances could make or break careers, particularly for those in public office. "This morning, Blaine acted like a different person."

"He was on the brink of death. That usually impacts personality."

"Perhaps."

After several long minutes, Bastian cleared his throat. "Do you think Wolf threatened Blaine not to disclose any valuable intel? They could be monitoring him."

"I'm sure they are. Lamb's in the wind, along with

Damian Bear."

"Didn't you shoot him?"

"Yes, but he escaped. And another hostage remains unaccounted for. The missing maid could be working with Wolf."

"One thing at a time." Bastian tapped more rapidly against the wheel. "Why does the Wolf Pack want to kill us? We are the only bloody negotiators working toward a resolution. If they wipe us out, no one will be clamoring to replace us. Wolf won't receive payment. The kidnapping will turn into murder. Perhaps it already has." Reaching for his phone, he hit a button, speed-dialing Hans. "Any news on Mrs. Blaine?"

"She's a tough bird, but the doctors won't know more until she wakes up," Hans said.

"Any uninvited visitors?"

"Just that pisser she married, and he didn't stay particularly long either. I spoke to the attending and wheedled some information out of her. They'll have a solid prognosis in a few days. Shall I make myself cozy until then?"

"Negative," Mercer interjected. "Blaine hired bodyguards. If he chooses, he can provide protection for his wife. Rendezvous at the safe house. We need a strategy." Pressing the disconnect button, Mercer waited for the inevitable question Bastian would ask.

"Am I to assume we're planning a tactical resolution?"

"We need a location first. We need access to Lamb and the rest of the released hostages. One of them will speak."

"Senator Blaine ought to possess enough clout to garner access to the consulate and his staff. Perhaps he can have us put on the guest list."

"Find out."

"Anything else, Jules?"

"The police are a suspicious lot, particularly Caho. They're in someone's pocket. After what Blaine said, I wouldn't be surprised if they are controlled by the cartel, or Caho's working for Wolf. Perhaps we should explore that avenue quietly."

"Well, since we're in such a destructive mood, why don't we just sod the Wolf Pack and go straight to the cartel for help? Don't they have methods of dealing with problems that arise? If the coppers aren't in their pocket, they'll eliminate them for us."

"Finally, you see reason."

"No."

Mercer could practically hear Bastian's eyes rolling. If the situation wasn't so dire, he might have been amused by his second-in-command's agitation. Before he could say or do anything else, the phone rang, and Mercer grabbed it.

"The audio and video are working on that bug you planted," Donovan said. "I have a visual of the hotel room. Blaine's on the phone with someone named Salvator. He's begging for more time and keeps promising to handle the situation without compromising their arrangement. Any idea what that's about? Do you think Salvator is part of Wolf's team?"

"Doubtful. Continue to monitor the feed for any visitors or calls. There's a possible third player coming onto the field. We'll need an ID, if possible."

"Yes, sir."

Bastian took the phone before Mercer decided to call in a preemptive airstrike of potential enemy strongholds.

Finally, the pair arrived at the flat. Without a word, they entered and set to work. Their first priority was updating the board with the latest intel and briefing Donovan on current developments.

Twenty minutes later, the proximity alarm buzzed. Bastian shot a quick glance at the monitor. Hans had returned. Without a word, the fourth member of their team slunk into the flat, hoping to remain unnoticed. However, his efforts were for nought when he entered the op center.

"You took your bloody time returning." Donovan lifted his gaze from the screen. "Were you tailed?"

"Nah, I was catching some tail." Smiling, Hans went into the kitchen and returned with a longneck. "What happened in there?"

"Don't ask," Bastian warned. "Things have drastically changed. Our latest intel is on the board. Familiarize yourself, then grab a pen, and map out enemy movement from this morning with respect to their approach and disappearance."

"Aye, aye," Hans said, his voice hitting a sarcastic note that drew Mercer's eyes from the file he was reading.

"Speak, Hans," Mercer said. "You have something to say. So speak."

"What about the boy? What are we doing to get him back?"

"This."

"What does chasing after some deported hostages or tracing opium trade lines have to do with saving an eleven-year-old?"

"It'll lead to the kidnappers and their location." Bastian sensed something bubbling beneath the surface. Hans could be mouthy and loud, but this was something else. "This is what we do."

"This *isn't* what we do." Hans stared at the aerial footage of the estate. "This morning, we should have been able to track the payment. The distraction was a waste. I should have seen who took the money and where they went."

"Why didn't you?" Mercer asked.

"Why didn't you? I'm not your dog. None of us are. We bloody well gave up everything for you. And I'm sick of being treated like an imbecile. A little gratitude would be nice, but I'd settle for a bit of respect. We're not perfect, but neither are you."

"Respect is earned." Mercer's eyes blazed, and Bastian stood, prepared to intervene should they come to blows. "This isn't a game, but you act like it is. You fuck around. You fail to take anything seriously, and because of that, the kidnapper is in the wind. He has the money and the child. We have nothing, except a woman who may never wake up. Screwing around gets people killed, but that's what you do."

"You would know. You're the expert at getting women killed."

Mercer was on his feet in a split second, but Bastian blocked his path. They stood at nearly the same height. Bastian stared fiercely into Mercer's murderous eyes.

"Julian, sit down." Bastian's voice was hard. "Do not let your anger cloud your better judgment. We failed today. People were hurt. No one else needs to be."

"Let him fight," Hans taunted.

Mercer lunged, and Bastian shoved him backward. "Donovan, get Hans out of here before I pop him myself." Giving Mercer another hard shove, Bastian glanced over his shoulder to see Donovan hauling an uncooperative Hans out of the room. The front door squeaked, and Bastian turned. Distracted, he wasn't prepared for Mercer to barrel into him, making a break for the front door and clawing at the knob. Yanking it open, he raced outside, slowing only when one of the vehicles peeled away.

Bastian followed him outside. Rubbing at his sore

side, he kicked Mercer in the back of the knee for good measure. "Really? And you wonder why people shoot at you. What were you going to do to him, Jules? Were you going to kill him?"

Mercer's eyes showed betrayal and loss, and instantly, his friend knew he was reliving the darkest moment of his life. His face contorted as he fought to keep it all inside.

"He shouldn't have said it," Bastian admitted, "but today was difficult for him too. You seem to forget his younger brother was killed by their abusive step-father. I believe he was around the same age as Nathaniel when it happened. I suspect that's why Hans is being rather insufferable. He blames himself for what went wrong. You didn't help matters."

Mercer barely nodded and went inside. Taking a seat, he flipped through the dossier, not seeing any of it. This wasn't working. It was rubbish. All of it.

When they had received word of the kidnapping and their services were requested, it sounded like a simple dispute. Hostages had been taken. Communication lines had been severed. Once those were reestablished, he and Bastian had tag-teamed the negotiation for fourteen hours. At the end, they should have come to a resolution, whether it was a tactical breach or a successful exchange. Instead, Wolf delayed again, and communication ceased for several hours. That piece of shit had used exhaustion and delay tactics to his advantage, which were typical tools K&R specialists employed.

Sure, Blaine's staff was freed, and they'd managed to rescue the senator. But Barbara Blaine was hanging on by a thread, and there was no way of knowing the fate of poor Nathaniel, who was alone with a group of psychos, not to mention the dead guard and the missing maid.

"Hans is right," Mercer declared, his voice barely above a whisper.

Bastian looked up, seeing the forlornness masking the bitter anger and resentment that permeated Mercer's soul. "Well, you could start treating us with a bit more respect, mate. A thank you every once in a while would go a long way." Bastian cracked a smile, hoping to calm the waters.

"Not about that, Bas."

"Oh, so you think we are your dogs?" Sensing he wouldn't be able to shake Mercer from his dour mood, he sighed. "We each have our reasons for being here. It doesn't matter what Hans said. We might have given the two finger salute to her majesty when you were canned, but we're here because something drives us to be here. For Hans, that's saving a few young lads from a gruesome fate. When it doesn't go well, he gets mouthy. More so than usual. That doesn't make him right, but it doesn't make you right either."

"I don't care. Right does not concern me. We need to save the boy. We failed his mum."

"She could recover."

Mercer reached for the phone and dialed Donovan. "Put Hans on." After a moment, Hans came on the line. "We need to punish those responsible. You did not cause this."

"I agree." Hans let out an audible exhale. "I shouldn't have implied that..."

"It's fine," Mercer said. "Return to the flat. We need to plan."

"All right, we'll just finish this pint first."

Mercer looked at Bastian. "We'll join you."

EIGHTEEN

"For Barbara." Donovan toasted to the woman in the ICU.

"Don't start that shit," Bastian warned. "If we start toasting to those injured or lost over the years, the drinking will never end."

"I believe that's the point." Hans took a large glug from his glass. He had been cautious around Mercer since the scene at the flat. The commander said it was fine, and in all the years they'd served together, he didn't know Mercer to go back on his word. However, he'd been keeping his distance since the four rendezvoused at the outdoor pub, if you could call this tropical locale a pub. Getting up to fetch another drink, he returned with two. Placing one on the table in front of Mercer, he took a seat beside him. "Jules, I want these bastards."

"So do I." Mercer picked up the glass and nodded his thanks. "We shall have them."

"How?"

Mercer shrugged. "Any suggestions?"

"I checked the waters earlier, but there are no signs of our stolen dinghy," Donovan said.

"I don't believe Wolf and the boy are on the island," Hans admitted. "When I was scouting for the second Land Rover, I realized just how small this place is. I believe Wolf's men are here, watching, observing, and reporting, but there are over two hundred tiny islands within a hundred kilometers. The boy could be anywhere."

"Blaine didn't tell you where he was kept?" Donovan asked.

"Oh, he told us. His memory was stellar when describing the takeover of the estate. Masked men with rifles burst inside, separated the family from the staff, and kept the senator secluded in his office until he was dragged out and forced to stay on the lower deck of the speedboat with his wife and son, and then his recollection gets dicey. It is possible he doesn't know, doesn't remember, or they never left the boat," Bastian said. "Then again, Jules thinks it's rubbish."

"Why aren't we storming the consulate? We need access to the victims. We need to interrogate the Butcher." Hans snorted. "What kind of shite name is Lamb anyway? Is that supposed to be apropos, like he's a wolf in sheep's clothing?"

"Then shouldn't he be named Wolf instead of the bastard calling the shots?" Donovan asked.

Hans downed the rest of his drink. A few more and this conversation would seem brilliant. "The police are uncooperative. They never even bothered to look into any of the allegations we made or the very obvious kidnapping. They want to hinder our ability, so why haven't they issued warrants for our arrests? We could be kidnappers or murderers. What about the bloke who was killed and left in our hotel?" He looked at Mercer. "You practically assaulted that bobby for taking your weapon."

"That was no assault," Mercer protested, but the wheels were spinning. "It stands to reason whoever controls this island controls the police force and is assisting the kidnappers."

"Intentionally or coincidentally?" Bastian sighed. "It must be the cartel."

"Didn't you say Blaine bartered some under the table deal with them?" Donovan asked.

"Yes." Mercer finished his drink.

"Lest we forget, Blaine insisted his underworld partner wouldn't need to go to these lengths to make a withdrawal," Bastian said. "The only link between the cartel and the kidnapping is the fact Blaine was summoned here by his unnamed associate for a meeting that was conveniently canceled."

"How do we know the Wolf Pack wasn't hired by the cartel?" Hans asked. "It sounds like some bullshit story to me. It's too easy."

"We don't know." Mercer focused on a woman several tables away.

"What would a cartel have to gain by hiring former PMCs to hijack the trade routes? That's counterintuitive. They would be competing entities." Bastian popped a handful of pretzels into his mouth. "The fields were destroyed, signifying the need for Blaine to meet with the cartel leader to explain the destruction. We should work under the assumption Wolf burned the crop to get Blaine here."

"Who else has a vested interest in the region?" Donovan asked.

"It's rife with resources—opium, discarded artillery, metals, minerals, oil. The place is a powder keg, just waiting for someone to do something dodgy," Bastian said.

"Then why aren't we doing something to figure this

out? At the very least, we should verify the funds in the numbered accounts and get inside the consulate," Hans said. "Any one of the released captives might be able to shed some insight into this."

"The senator is using his clout to open official channels and get us access. We have a meeting scheduled in the morning with some PR twit. However, due to the circumstances, the consulate officials have deemed this a local matter and one that American citizens should not be forced to further subject themselves to if they do not wish." Bastian swirled the melting ice cubes in his empty glass. "Not every hostage is a US citizen, but we have no idea where any of the others went. They vanished, even the ones in the hospital."

"Caho did this." Mercer's focus remained on the woman and her companions. "He's covering it up."

"Like I said, he's working with the kidnapper," Hans muttered. "Why don't we get him to talk?"

"It could jeopardize the boy and lessen the chance of recovery," Bastian said.

"Do you really believe there will be a recovery? Come on, Bas, the only recovery we'll be lucky to make is fishing the boy's body out of the water." Hans looked away, gripping the glass firmly in his hand.

"It's your call." Bastian waited for Mercer to respond. After a moment, he snapped his fingers in front of Julian's face. "Commander, are you still with us?" Turning to see what had Mercer's attention, Bastian snorted, and a smile crept onto his face. "She's pretty. Why don't you give it a go?"

Flicking his gaze to Bastian, Mercer cocked an eyebrow. "What?"

"The bird," Bastian said.

"She's one of Blaine's bloody staffers." Mercer turned his attention to Hans. "Didn't you save her from drowning?"

Hans narrowed his eyes. She looked different dry and dressed in club attire, but it was her.

"And that tosser two tables over, that's the arsehole with the camera," Donovan said. "What are they doing here?"

"This is a bar. They probably fancied a drink," Hans said. "Are there any other familiar faces in the crowd?"

The four men scanned their surroundings but didn't recognize anyone else. Bastian eyed the area around them, realizing the outdoor bar left them at a disadvantage. They were exposed. The possibility that a member of the Wolf Pack was outside their current range of sight but monitoring them or planning an ambush was unsettling, particularly when two possible leads on determining the boy's location were drinking several meters away.

"Keep in mind, they might be innocent. If she's one of the caretakers for Blaine's holiday home, she wouldn't have been sent to the consulate with the others," Bastian said.

"Be that as it may, that wanker with the camera is the reason I took this knock to the noggin'." Donovan diverted his gaze, hoping the man wouldn't notice him. "I'd prefer to take the lady, unless you want things to get loud and a little messy."

"Bastian, Donovan, stay on the woman," Mercer instructed. "Lure her away. Try to do it quietly. Hans and I will deal with the paparazzo."

"Are you sure that's wise?" Bastian asked but dropped the question with one look from Mercer. "What are we doing with them once we have them?"

"Take them back to the safe house. We'll question them there, but be careful. This could be a trap." Mercer stood and lifted his empty glass. Getting a refill provided the perfect excuse to go to the bar and get closer to their male target. "I'll flush him out. He ought to recognize me."

"Aye." Hans eased back in his seat, watching their surroundings like a hungry cat studying a fish tank.

Once Mercer was positioned at the bar, awaiting the bartender's attention, Bastian strode through the array of tables and smiled at the woman. Unlike the other men on the team, Bastian had the innate ability to appear the least threatening. Perhaps he knew how to use his charms or utilize his uncanny skills at reading body language and facial tics to guide his words. Either way, he was invited to join the woman and her friends. Once he was seated, Mercer moved away from the bar toward his intended target.

"Nice night." Mercer leaned his elbows against the high-top table, facing away from the man.

"Sure," the guy said, not paying much attention to whom he was speaking.

"You have a choice." Mercer smiled, lifting his still empty glass to his lips, more for show than anything else. "You can do what I say and not be harmed, or the next few hours will be unpleasant."

"Dude, what the f—" The man spun, recognizing Mercer instantly. Bolting to the left, he knocked over the chair and made a beeline through the narrow spaces between the tables.

Hans moved sideways, anticipating his prey's direction, and raced past the enclosed area. He gave the fleeing man a wide berth but kept him in his sights. Mercer pursued through the crowd, pushing people aside and bumping into several chairs and tables on the way. As soon as the man was beyond the boundaries of the outdoor bar, he burst into a sprint, heading toward the water.

Tackling him, Hans and the man rolled in the sand.

After a few moments, the man stopped struggling. Hans twisted the man's arm behind his back and hauled him to his feet. "Were you planning to swim for it? Did you think you'd have better luck with the sharks?"

"What do you people want? I didn't do anything to you." Spotting Mercer, he gulped down some air. "You're that crazy son of a bitch who interrogated those people on the beach." He struggled to get a better look at Hans. "And you're the one who nearly drowned them." He sucked in a breath and screamed at the top of his lungs. "Help. Someone, help me. They're going to kill me. Help."

"Silence," Mercer said, but the man continued to yell. Mercer punched him in the stomach hard enough to knock the wind out of him. The man let out a strangled yelp and doubled over. "Do not do that again."

"Jules, we might want to take this party elsewhere," Hans suggested, looking back at the growing crowd of onlookers.

"Come on." Mercer grabbed the man's free arm and dragged him to his feet. "Do not put up a fight. Do not make a peep."

Making a show of brushing the sand off the guy, Hans gave a friendly wave. "Wave to the crowd, mate. Big smile. Big smile." It was dark, and no one could see facial expressions from that distance, but the man complied anyway, feeling the barrel of Hans' handgun pressed against his ribcage. "Very good. Now we're going to take a ride. If you want to see the sun rise again, you will behave."

After the onlookers decided it was nonsense yelled by some drunken idiot, they want back to minding their own business. Mercer and Hans walked the man past the bar.

Unlocking only the driver's side doors, Hans shoved the man into the back seat and pushed him across, glad for child safety locks. Taking a seat behind Mercer, Hans trained his weapon on the captive. Mercer got behind the wheel, gave the area a final scan, and started the engine. Once they were moving at a steady speed with no other vehicles in sight, Mercer glanced in the rearview mirror, studying the man's expression.

"Who are you?"

"Alexander Loren." The man's eyes flicked from Hans' face to the gun. "Who are you?"

"Why were you taking pictures of my team and the hostages?" Mercer asked.

"What?"

"That morning when those ten people were saved from drowning, you were in the market with your phone, taking photographs. Explain." Hans' eyes grew dark.

"That's what I do," Loren said. "I'm a photojournalist."

"Then you'd have a real camera, not some shitty smart phone. What story were you reporting? What do you know about those people?"

"Nothing," Loren said. "I told the other guy the same thing."

"The other guy?" Mercer asked. "Are you responsible for attacking my friend?"

"He attacked me first," Loren protested. "And I didn't do that. He lured me to his car and forced me into his hotel room. I don't know who hit him, but when they jumped him, I got out of there." He wiped the back of his hand across his mouth. "I'll ask again, who are you people?"

Mercer and Hans remained silent. It was too soon to tell if the man was lying, but once they were back at the safe house, it'd be easier to ask questions and verify his answers. "Take his phone," Mercer said, watching as Hans reached into the man's pocket and removed the device. "Turn it off and remove the battery until Bastian has a chance to make sure it's not being tracked."

Hans lowered his weapon, needing both hands to remove the battery cover, and Loren made a move. The photojournalist headbutted Hans and clawed for the gun. However, the wannabe paparazzo was smart enough to know he had been bested. When the cold steel of Mercer's handgun pressed into Loren's forehead, the man raised his hands and leaned away from Hans, releasing his grip on the gun.

"Wanker." Hans picked up the weapon and cracked Loren across the face. "Try something dodgy and see what happens." He finished removing the battery and pocketed the device. "Thanks, Jules. I needed that extra hand."

NINETEEN

"Where are we?" Loren's eyes darted over the equipment and printouts that covered the desk while Hans hauled him past their op center and into the kitchen. "What do you plan on doing with me?"

Mercer pulled out one of the kitchen chairs and placed it in the center of the room. Securing Loren's hands behind the chair back with a pair of handcuffs, Mercer waited for Hans to bind their prisoner's legs and body to the chair before circling their potential foe.

"You said you're a photojournalist. Where do you work?" Mercer nodded to Hans, and the other man went into the op center and returned with a tablet. Reaching into their captive's pocket, Mercer removed Loren's wallet and looked through it until he found a photo ID. "Alexander Loren of Miami, Florida. I didn't realize U.S. papers reported on tiny island nations in the Caribbean."

"It depends." Loren's glare could have hardened the melting icecaps. "News travels."

"Where are your press credentials?" Mercer flipped through the wallet again, tossing out the contents as he went.

"I never said I worked for a paper."

Mercer was used to being stonewalled by enemy insurgents, not tourists in Hawaiian shirts. "The truth. Now."

"I'm a photojournalist. That's it. What does that have to do with anything? What do you want from me?" Loren asked, repeating his earlier statement as if it were his name, rank, and serial number.

"This is going nowhere." Hans leaned against the counter while searching for usable intel on this paparazzo wannabe. "I'd suggest you fess up. You already made a sucky first impression, and now you're doing nothing but pissing us off. I don't know any photojournalists who would do anything as ballsy as what you tried in the back of the car. Who are you?"

"I'm Alexander Loren. I'm nobody. What are you going to do with me? What do you want?"

"We want the truth." Hans glanced at Mercer who was intrigued by the broken glass littering the floor. "You should know the commander isn't particularly patient. So I'll ask once more, why were you snapping photos?"

"That's just something I do."

"Even if you don't work for a newspaper, you must work for some media outlet. Where are your press credentials?" Mercer repeated.

"I don't have any."

"And you expect us to believe you're a photojournalist?" Hans snorted. "C'mon, you can come up with a better lie than that."

"I'm not lying. I swear to god, I'm a photojournalist."

"No, you're not. You have nothing on your person

to verify your story." Hans lowered the tablet. "Just name the news station, and we'll sort this out."

Loren scowled. "I'm not telling you shit."

"You will." Mercer lingered closer, sizing up his captive.

"Perhaps he's an intelligence agent," Hans said. "Albeit a bloody stupid one, unless he's on someone's payroll and they didn't bother providing a decent cover."

"Why don't you tell me who you people are?" Loren said.

"How do you know John Wolf?" Mercer lifted the bottom portion of a broken tumbler from the floor. He held up the glass, inspecting the jagged rim and smiling.

"Who?"

"Wolf." Mercer pressed the jagged edge of the glass into Loren's crotch. "Tell me what I want to know, or you'll have no use for the condoms I tossed out of your wallet."

Loren tried to wriggle backward, but the chair didn't budge. Mercer pressed down a little harder, knowing the glass wasn't sharp enough to penetrate the guy's trousers without excessive force. However, it was enough to scare him into talking.

"I don't know anyone by that name," Loren yelped.

Scrunching his face into a cringe, Hans cleared his throat. "Maybe he's telling the truth."

"That would be a first," Mercer said. "He is no photojournalist."

"I am too." Loren's petulant insistence was met with a searing look. "I'm freelance. I blog."

"Blog?" Mercer eased the pressure off the man's genitals, staring fiercely into the guy's eyes. "Hans?"

"Give me a minute." Hans entered something on the tablet and scrolled through the pages. "I'm not finding anything."

"Too bad." Mercer pushed down harder, eliciting a pained grunt from the man.

"Loren's Lair," their captive screamed.

"Wait," Hans moved to stand beside Mercer, "is this a blog?"

Mercer skimmed the webpage dedicated to wildlife photos, underwater coral reef images, and articles about pollution and destruction of the environment. "*Loren's Lair, insight into our changing habits and habitat*," Mercer read aloud, giving the man a bewildered look. "You're a bleeding idiot. What does this have to do with hostages? Who hired you to take those photos?"

"I'm a freelance reporter," Loren said. "If I see something intriguing, I snap a shot."

Hans whispered his thoughts into Mercer's ear. Despite the crappy webpage, too many coincidences surrounded their captive. He had been in the right place at the right time one too many times, and he reacted and behaved like someone with training and experience. "Number one rule of spycraft, don't waver from the lie."

Mercer had no doubt this man was involved, but he could be working for anyone. The cartel, the Wolf Pack, or even Senator Blaine. "Where's the boy?"

"What boy? You guys are crazy. Who do you think I am? What are you talking about? I proved who I was. What more do you want? Look, take whatever you want. If you're going to kill me, just get it over with."

Replacing the battery in Loren's phone, Hans powered it on, hoping it wasn't being tracked. After being denied access to the contents, he went around the chair and forced Loren's thumb against the screen. Everything on the phone backed Loren's story. He had photos of sea life, native animals, plants, local residents, the poverty and devastation that wreaked havoc on parts of the island, and the stark contrast with the sections filled with touristy resorts. The few photographs he found from the hostage rescue were distance shots of the group. Nothing close-up or suspicious and none of Mercer or the team.

"Jules, perhaps we've got it wrong."

"Doubtful." Mercer tossed the broken glass into the sink. "This twat led Donovan into an ambush." Grabbing the nearest chair, Mercer sat in front of Loren. "I don't believe you. Two things are about to happen. One, you will be made blind and deaf. Two, you are about to experience a level of pain you didn't believe existed. Last chance. Where's the boy?"

Loren stared at Mercer, and with a level of certainty he had no right to possess given the circumstances, he asked, "Who are you?"

"Get the equipment ready." Mercer pushed his chair away.

"Commander?" Hans didn't move, and Mercer gave him a sideways look. "This wanker won't see morning. Do you care if I give it a go before we make a mess?"

Mercer shrugged.

"You're in charge?" Loren's eyes focused on Mercer. "Military. Private?" He smiled. "Must be since I didn't hear news of a war brewing. Obviously, not police. Well, with the way they function around here, I wouldn't put it past them, but they don't seem competent enough to successfully torture out a confession. You do."

"Then you better start talking," Hans said, leery of the switch their captive just flipped.

"I'm a freelance reporter." He cocked his head to the side. Then in a single move, he freed his wrists and leapt backward, knocking the chair to the ground hard enough that it broke. He remained in motion, sliding out of the ropes and letting the momentum carry him to his feet. He grabbed what remained of the back of the chair and swung at Hans.

The chair fragment hit Hans square in the jaw, and Loren lunged forward, removing Hans' side arm in one quick move. Shifting behind the dazed shooter, Loren held the gun against Hans' throat, leaving no room to struggle or resist.

Mercer trained his weapon on Loren. How the man moved with that much speed and precision was unbelievable. It was practically superhuman. This man was no photojournalist.

"Don't." Loren inched further behind Hans to obscure himself from the trajectory of Mercer's bullet. "Lower your weapon."

"No." Losing a member of the team wasn't acceptable, but war was about sacrifice. And Alexander Loren just declared war. "You kill him. I kill you."

"It's that simple?" Loren pressed the muzzle of the gun harder into Hans' neck.

"If anything happens to him, you lose everything." Mercer's finger remained steady on the trigger, his breath slowing in anticipation of firing.

Hans eyed Mercer, knowing precisely when and how the commander would fire. "I'd listen to him. He negotiates for a living. You're outwitted here."

"Negotiates?" Loren asked. "You aren't military?"

"We used to be," Hans said, deciding talking was a nice way to delay the inevitable. "Special Air Service until we gave the Queen the royal salute. Now we negotiate with shitheads like you. Frankly, we were better off with her majesty."

Mercer tapped his finger gently against the handle three times. He was counting down. Hans knew to spin to his right when the count reached one.

"Former British military." Loren processed the newly acquired information.

"Where'd you think we got the accents?" Hans remained transfixed on Mercer's finger. Two.

"Shit." Loren held the gun up, raising his hands. Hans grabbed it, elbowing him, and slamming his chest down against the table. "Don't shoot. You've got it all wrong. I had it all wrong."

"What are you chattering about?" Hans gave the man's arm a thorough twist, half a second away from breaking it or snapping a few tendons. "Speak quickly."

"I was sent to this island on Senator Blaine's behalf. I'm security."

"Security?" Mercer had yet to lower his weapon. Given how this man had moved only seconds earlier, he wasn't willing to risk a repeat performance.

"Yes. I wasn't at the estate the morning it was overrun by mercs, so I've been observing from a distance. I thought you and your men were part of the team that led the assault."

Nothing about the situation or Loren's previous denials or current statement resonated as truthful. Mercer nodded to Hans. With a resounding crack and a surprised yelp, the bone broke. Loren cursed, cradling his arm against his stomach while Mercer kept his gun trained on the man.

"Why did you do that? I'm telling you the truth." Loren's eyes were wet, a sign of the sudden unexpected pain, but he didn't behave like a normal human who just had his arm broken. Alexander Loren had experience and training. He might be part of the senator's security detail, but he was something far deadlier.

"I've spoken to the senator. He did not mention additional security," Mercer said.

"He doesn't know. Honest to god, he doesn't know. I'm with the Secret Service."

"Rubbish." Mercer's head spun from the lies. "Detain him. And this time, make sure he can't escape. Break his other arm and both his legs if need be."

"No, wait," Loren pleaded as Hans forced him into another kitchen chair, this time going to the extremes to bind him with an excessive amount of duct tape before retrieving a bag containing restraints, a hood, and several other unpleasant items. "You need my help. You can't do this. You don't know where to look. You don't know who you're up against."

"What can you offer?" Mercer watched the black hood slide over the man's face. Finally, he relaxed, lowering his weapon. With a broken arm and enough restraints to shackle a bear, maintaining a bead on their captive wasn't necessary.

The words came out muffled from beneath the hood. "I can tell you precisely what they want."

"Go on." Mercer looked at Hans who was rubbing his jaw. A large welt had already erupted. Soon, a dark bruise would follow. It was just the two of them, and neither had any idea what to believe.

"Not until I have some assurances you'll let me go."

"If you can't provide valuable intel, you will be killed. That's the only assurance you have," Hans said. "I'll do you in myself. A bit of payback for that chair and attacking my mate."

For several moments, Loren didn't speak. Then he let out a muffled grunt after unsuccessfully struggling against the bindings. "They want to take over the drug trade in the Middle East, and the senator has the power to make it happen."

"Who are they?" Mercer asked.

"Untie me."

Mercer turned his back. Their captive would become desperate soon enough. They already broke his arm. Now they just needed to break his will.

.

TWENTY

After dialing Blaine, Mercer spoke briefly to the senator, hoping to discover any truth to the claim Loren was part of the Secret Service. Blaine practically laughed, acknowledging only under specific and special circumstances would a senator ever be given a detail. However, given the situation, Blaine phoned his assistant, double-checked the facts, and provided Mercer with verification that no Secret Service agents had been assigned for his protection.

"Who do you think he is?" Hans asked. Their captive was still bound in the kitchen where Mercer and Hans could maintain eyes on him, but they had placed noise canceling headphones over his ears and blasted death metal through the speakers. "My money's on an intelligence operative. CIA? NSA? Then again, maybe that damn American accent is bullshit. Middle East drug trade could indicate Russians. Spetsnaz? GRU? Those blokes were pretty pissed about the 1970s Afghanistan thing. Well, the whole Cold War thing really. And now, with American politics being a shitstorm, Russia looks like the perfect culprit to blame. Then again, drugs tend to follow cartels, which could be the Bratva, depending on circumstances." The close call had made him chattier than usual, and he spouted out whatever thoughts came to mind, despite his swollen jaw. "Then again, we are south of the equator. Most of the American drug trade originates from below their southern border. Loren could be working for any of them really. Maybe he's a hired gun for Blaine's unnamed associate. Maybe you should ring the senator again and ask."

"I don't believe an accurate response would be forthcoming."

"If we assume Occam's razor, my wager is on a corrupt DEA agent. Former SpecOps turned rogue DEA agent. Do you even think Alexander Loren is his real name?"

Mercer didn't give a flying shag about politics, let alone how the Americans were mucking up the world. He wanted to save the boy. The rest was irrelevant. "Where's Bastian?"

"He and Donovan should be along soon."

"Watch him." Mercer pointed to the bound man before vacating the room. Scanning Loren's driver's license, he entered the image into the computer. While the facial recognition software hummed along, he did a database search for the name. Then he dialed a few of his former mates from military intelligence, asking that they perform a search for any military or police assets who fit Loren's description. When the intel wasn't immediately forthcoming, Mercer dialed another number.

"Parker," a female voice answered.

"I'm sending you a copy of a Florida driver's license. The man claims to be a member of the Secret

Service, but I have no way of verifying this. You can."

"You expect me to believe Bastian doesn't possess the ability to bypass our firewalls and get whatever he pleases?" She paused for a split second. "Is he okay?"

"He isn't here. I need this now."

"So you called me? Am I your new phone-a-friend? Because I'd rather not have that distinction."

"You're an FBI agent. This can't wait."

"All right. Give me a minute." After several moments of silence, except for the faint echo of typing, she let out an amused snort. "Loren's information is classified. It's beyond my clearance level. All I can tell you is he was army. From the way this reads, he's probably working for one of our agencies, but there's no mention of Secret Service. I'm guessing he's a spook. Black ops, off the books."

"We already determined as much."

"Then you shouldn't have wasted the dime on the long distance."

The silence answered her question.

"Julian, I'm still gathering information, but I haven't found anything new on your wife's case since the last time we spoke. I won't drop the ball. I promised I'd contact you when I have something. You have my word. You don't have to come up with excuses to check on my progress."

"Fine." He disconnected, brushing off her accusation. Unfortunately, somewhere in his psyche, her words rang true. But there were more pressing matters to deal with, so Mercer returned to the kitchen. "He's an American spy. That's all we know. Bastian will have to find out more once he gets here." Mercer checked the time. "It shouldn't have taken him this long to secure the woman and bring her here. What do you think is keeping them?"

"I'll give Donovan a ring and find out." Hans' call

went unanswered. "Perhaps we ought to proceed with interrogating this chap and then set out in search of our mates."

Mercer yanked the hood from Loren's head and removed the headphones. "Nathaniel Blaine has yet to be returned. His mother is clinging to life, and his father is a bastard. I do not intend to allow harm to befall the boy. The longer this continues, the more likely the outcome will be grave. Stop being a hindrance, or you will be the first to experience my wrath."

"Damn, I was just getting into the beat." Loren blinked a few times as his eyes adjusted to the light. "This is pointless. We're on the same side. Don't you realize that?"

"What's your objective?" Hans asked.

"To ensure Senator Blaine's safe return. Much like the reason you're here."

"Blaine appears to be safe," Mercer said. "If your mission was to ensure his safety, you would be with him now, not drinking at a beachside bar. Nor would you be taking photographs of the rescued hostages. Who sent you here?"

"I told you I'm part of the senator's protection detail," Loren insisted.

"Funny, you must have missed picture day at the Secret Service," Hans said. "You don't work for them. You aren't some bloody journalist. You've got one more shot at this. I suggest you work a bit harder to make this lie believable."

"I'm here to ensure Blaine's safe return."

"Eeeee, wrong answer." Hans mimicked a game show buzzer. "Shall I show the man what he's won?"

Mercer nodded, and Hans lifted a mallet, swinging into Loren's already broken arm. The American howled in pain. Luckily, they were far enough from the civilized world that no one would hear him. This was the precise reason they rented a small secluded beach cottage.

After several curses and stifled cries, Loren glared at Hans. "That is the truth."

"Shall I take out the other shoulder?" Hans asked, his eyes on fire. "We don't appreciate your lies."

"That's not a lie," Loren spat. "Does it even matter? Tell me what you want me to say, and I'll say it. Isn't that how this works? You can't beat a confession out of someone because everyone has a breaking point. At some point, a man will say or do anything to get the torture to stop."

"And we reached your breaking point this quickly?" Mercer asked.

Loren didn't respond.

"Kneecap then?" Hans asked.

"Please," Loren whispered.

"Why is Blaine so important?" Mercer asked. "You said they need him to take over the Middle East drug trade. Who are they? What are you trying to stop?"

"It's my understanding PMC Wolf and his former unit were recruited to discover Blaine's cartel connection and undermine the brokered deal," Loren finally said.

"Were you sent here to stop him?" Mercer asked, and Loren nodded. "Who sent you?"

"I'm not at liberty to say." Loren sounded like every spy in every movie Mercer had ever seen.

"We're on the same side," Hans mocked. "What is your objective?"

"Blaine's safety. I already told you that. I'll cooperate. Just stop this. We can help each other."

Mercer leaned against the counter. "Where are they? Who do they work for? Where's the boy?"

"I don't know where they are." He dragged in a

ragged breath. "And I can't tell you who hired them."

"Can't or won't?" Hans asked.

"Bollocks." Mercer held out his hand, taking the weapon from Hans. "I don't think you'll be able to serve your agency as a cripple." He dragged the chair away from the wall, running the mallet against Loren's back. "If I hit here, you'll lose all function beneath the waist. If I hit here, you lose your arms too. A little higher and you won't be able to breathe on your own. What's it going to be?"

Loren bucked, struggling from side to side. "You asshole. Aren't you supposed to be one of the good guys?"

"My purpose is to save the boy. The rest doesn't matter." Mercer tapped the mallet lightly against the middle of the man's back. Truthfully, he had no intention of crippling him. Torture to that extreme wouldn't result in answers. It would only take away their captive's will to live and all hope of seeing the outside world again. Without those things, Loren would refuse to cooperate and any chance of this being a useful conversation would come to a crashing halt. Inevitably, if they were forced to eliminate the man, it would be quick and fairly painless.

"I can neither confirm nor deny my involvement in any active U.S. operations that may be underway to prevent a change of power in the Middle East," Loren sputtered, sounding like he was testifying before a Senate oversight committee. He wasn't exactly ready to crack, but his resolve to remain unhelpful was fading.

"Does Blaine know you're here?" Hans asked.

"I don't believe so."

"Is the senator aware of the situation regarding the reason behind the kidnapping and the actual ransom demand?" Hans asked, trying a more direct approach.

"I believe he's been informed. You would know better than I would." Loren struggled to see Mercer, who was still positioned behind him. "As of four hours ago, Blaine had yet to initiate any changes to the procedures in place."

"How would the shift in the drug trade commence?" Mercer asked.

"I cannot—"

Hans sighed dramatically. "Confirm or deny. Right-o. We have no interest here other than saving the boy. We need some solid facts. Now."

Mercer tapped Loren's spine a little harder, and Loren shuddered. Their captive wanted to live. Although his long-term goal in life appeared to be annoying Mercer.

"We know this has something to do with government contracts, the use of private military, and Blaine's vote. Other than that, we know a group of mercs, led by Wolf, committed a frontal assault on Blaine's estate, released his staff, and took the family to an undisclosed location. Since then, Blaine and his wife were released, but the boy has yet to be found. Negotiations have halted. Blaine is of no use, and neither are you," Mercer said. "That's everything we know. It's your turn to share. Why were you photographing the victims?"

"In order to identify enemy infiltrators."

"Finally." Hans took the mallet as Mercer came around to face the bound man.

"We need names." Mercer left no room for debate.

"Damian Bear was at the market that morning. Theodore Lamb was among those shackled. I suspect a woman hired to clean the senator's estate might be working with them. I followed her to the bar. Before I could make my approach, you intervened."

"Is she dangerous?"

Loren shrugged.

"Commander, we should go," Hans said.

Mercer went into the op center and scanned the records they had. "There's no mention of a female working with the team. Who is she?"

"I believe she was placed inside the senator's estate by the party who wants to take control of power in the Middle East. We know her only by a codename, Jezebel," Loren said.

"Sounds like rubbish." Mercer's glare failed to loosen Loren's lips further. "Have you spoken to Lamb since the rescue?"

"Answer him," Hans insisted, hefting the mallet higher.

"He escaped," Loren admitted. "He and the rest of the hostages were supposed to be shuttled to the consulate. An asset there was conducting background checks, hoping to determine potential risks and separate Lamb and any others from the group, but Lamb was released from police custody before my people had a chance to intercept."

"Your people." Mercer narrowed his eyes. "How large is your team?"

"I told you I'm with the government. I was working in concert with assets placed inside the consulate. They won't be pleased when I don't report back, and they'll be even less pleased to discover how poorly you've treated me. You really ought to let me go. Someone needs to stop Jezebel before she disappears or harms your friends."

"Stuff him in the cupboard," Mercer said. Once their guest had been made blind and deaf and was secured inside the pantry, Mercer turned to Hans. "It could be a lie."

"I agree, but we've lost communication with our teammates. Is it worth the risk?"

"No. Let's move out."

TWENTY-ONE

"Didn't Bas say he wanted to install trackers in our comms?" Hans asked as they headed toward the bar.

"It posed a risk. Wolf might have been able to use them against us." Mercer's grip on the steering wheel tightened, his mind on the boy. Wolf's silence didn't bode well. Despite Mr. and Mrs. Blaine's release, the circumstances were far from stellar. Mercer cast a sideways glance at Hans who was stroking the trigger on his handgun. "Do you believe anything Loren told us?"

"Some. It'd be easier to determine what parts are true if we knew with whom we are dealing."

"I concur."

"Obviously, we blindly trusted him enough to set out in search of our mates. If Loren is an American spy, I don't believe he's here to protect Blaine."

"He has an agenda," Mercer agreed. "Whatever that is requires the senator to remain breathing. If it didn't, there would be some sort of *accident*. No witnesses."

"Even the boy?"

Mercer nodded.

"And us?"

"Let them try."

"Great, just another name to add to the list." Hans checked the rearview mirror, but they weren't being followed. "Blaine's hiding something. You saw the boy's room, Jules. That bastard used his own son to hide the documents from those wankers. Who does that? I doubt whatever you found inside that dresser is legal. Someone went to great lengths to get it, and we have it in our possession. Why hasn't Wolf phoned with delivery instructions?"

"Like you said, Blaine is hiding something."

"I'm guessing it has to do more with his underhanded deals than some PMC's salary. This is a clusterfuck. We have the cartel, the Wolf Pack, either rogue operatives or some clandestine agency, and the island's police force circling like vultures. Did I miss anyone?"

"Jezebel." Mercer eyed the empty road ahead of them and checked the side and rear mirrors. For a moment, he thought he caught a glimpse of a vehicle running dark behind them. He executed another turn, cognizant of any reflecting lights. "Do you see anyone behind us?"

Hans' eagle-sharp vision didn't detect anything. After a half mile, he turned back around, paying close attention to the side mirror. "No."

"Nerves." Mercer let out an exhale. "Bastian and Donovan should have gotten to the safe house before us. Something's not right."

"Perhaps the bloody bobbies know where they are." Hans jerked his chin at the flashing lights outside the beachside bar. A few nosy islanders lurked near the patrol car, speaking quietly to one another. "Should we ask the natives?"

Reluctantly, Mercer stopped the car twenty meters from the police vehicle and stepped out. Several tire tracks were carved in the sand, leading to the outdoor patio. Whatever happened had already been cleaned up. "We're too late."

"Jules?" Hans' gaze raked over the tracks and came to a stop in the middle of the outdoor bar. The area was vacant, except for the bartender and two patrolmen. One of the officers was questioning the bartender. The other appeared to be cleaning up a mess. "You don't think...no." Hans shook his head, dismissing the errant thought before it could be verbalized. He scanned the dark sky, noting the outline of buildings and nearby rooftops. "We didn't scout beforehand. They could have been set up anywhere. We could have walked into an ambush and never realized it. Those buildings would provide perfect vantage points for sniper fire."

Mercer went to the police car. Opening the door, he took a seat behind the wheel and rummaged through the paperwork covering the passenger's seat. Thankfully, the officers had left the call sheet and preliminary report behind.

A single female had been gunned down. Dispatch received several calls of shots fired and requests for medical assistance. No one knew where the shots originated, but two men had been seen speaking to the woman and her friends seconds before the commotion.

Mercer stepped out of the car. "I know where our teammates are."

"Were they killed?"

"No. The police have them." Mercer returned to the car and slammed the door, barely waiting for Hans to join him. Giving the mirror a final glance, he started the engine. Something didn't feel right, but he couldn't figure out what was out of place. He stomped on the accelerator and prepared for another confrontation with Capt. Caho.

A few seconds later, his cell phone rang. It was a forwarded call from the command center. "Take the wheel," Mercer instructed, feeling as though he needed both hands free to deal with the kidnapper.

"Miss me yet?" Wolf asked. "We haven't spoken in hours. As a negotiator you must be beside yourself, unsure what to do or how to proceed. Perhaps we should have another gabfest."

"What do you want?"

"I want Blaine's answer. Is he prepared to meet our demands?"

"I will need time to confer with the senator."

Wolf let out a bored yawn. "I'm growing tired of the boy. You have one hour to provide an answer. Good luck convincing Blaine to save his only son."

Mercer took back the wheel, swerving and performing an illegal u-turn in the middle of the empty street.

"Where are we going now?" Hans asked.

"To get Blaine."

"And do what with him?"

"I haven't decided yet."

"What about our better halves? We have no way of knowing when Wolf will issue another ludicrous demand. We need our team whole in order to function properly." He sighed. "We haven't been doing a very good job of that lately, Jules. We should get them first."

"There isn't time."

"Then we make time. We can't afford not to."

The car screeched to a halt, and Mercer fought against his instinct to go ahead with the negotiation and instead turned the car back around, resuming course to the police station. Letting Hans take the wheel again, he dialed Blaine.

"Sir, I understand it's late, but the kidnapper has made another request. You will meet me outside the police station immediately. If you don't, I fear your son will not survive the night." Without waiting for the inevitable protest, Mercer disconnected. If the man had any bit of self-worth, he'd do as Mercer asked.

Parking in a visitor space out front, Mercer mentally prepared for another showdown with the island's law enforcement officers. It was imperative he remain professional and unemotional. However, he had no idea what might await him inside. The police had every reason to place him and Hans under arrest.

"How much cash do you have?" Mercer asked.

"Enough to buy our friends out of trouble."

"Good."

Mercer wasn't surprised to find the station nearly abandoned. An inspector stood over another officer's desk while the desk sergeant manned the front. Other than that, the place was empty. The desk sergeant gave Mercer a tired, aggravated look.

"You've got some balls showing your face here. How do you know we won't arrest you?"

"I'm looking for a couple of friends."

"Take a seat. The captain warned us you'd be stopping by." He dialed four numbers, spoke briefly, and hung up. "Captain Caho will be here shortly. Do you want something to drink?"

"I could go for a pint," Hans said.

Mercer eavesdropped on the conversation the inspector was having with the officer. The woman had been shot between the eyes. No one else had been harmed. Several shots had been fired into the bar.

Several glasses and bottles had been broken. In the resulting panic, additional property damage had been done.

"Busy night?" Mercer asked, but the desk sergeant didn't answer.

"Sounds like a professional hit," Hans whispered, eyeing the two cops. "My money says the shooter took out the woman before spraying the bar. The ruckus provided the perfect cover for escape. The shooter could have been one of those looky-loos standing around when we pulled up. Maybe that's why Wolf rang when he did."

"Maybe."

Emerging from the narrow hallway, Captain Caho sauntered over. "Mr. Mercer." He turned his attention to Hans. "And you are?"

"Hans Bauer."

"Captain Caho," he held out his hand, "nice to meet you." The sleazy car salesman schtick was back.

"Yeah, we'll see." Hans ignored Caho's extended hand. Instead, he held his position at Mercer's flank, keeping his eyes trained on the other cops.

"What brings you to my station this evening?" Caho asked. "Didn't you have enough last night?"

"I've misplaced a few friends," Mercer said.

"When did you see them last?"

"A couple hours ago." Mercer was uncertain of this man's game, but dodgy answers seemed to be part of the rhetoric. So he played along.

"I'd say it was less than two based on the reports I've read. Apparently, two men were involved in an altercation with a drunk. The drunk alleged these men planned to kill him. However, after a brief tussle near the water, the man changed his tune, and the three went off together. Bygones, I suppose." Caho's smile resembled that of a Cheshire cat. "Did I happen to mention those two men had been in the company of two other men prior to that incident? And this second pair was in the presence of a young woman who was murdered in the middle of a crowded bar. I find it disconcerting you and your friends have such bad luck. First, a kidnapping, then a murder inside your hotel room, several altercations with my officers, and now a second murder." Caho made a tsk sound. "I can't continue to turn a blind eye to the crimes that have befallen my island. So Mr. Mercer, would you like to step into my office and have a nice long chat concerning what's really going on here?"

"Are my associates in custody?"

"C'mon," Hans drawled, "how 'bout a little tit for tat?"

Caho smirked. "Tell me why my island has turned into a battleground."

"Hell if I know." Hans' gaze darted toward the hallway from which Caho emerged. "Isn't it the job of the police to provide protection and security?"

"Your friends aren't here. No one was arrested. By the time my men arrived, they had fled. Unless you clear this up, you better hope I don't find them. Because if I do, I can't guarantee their safety. We aren't in the business of protecting killers," Caho said.

"That's precisely what you're doing." Before Mercer could say anything else, Harry Blaine burst through the front door with his bodyguards in tow. "Excuse me."

Stepping away from Caho, Mercer nodded to a frantic Blaine. Someone had finally lit a fire beneath the senator. Too bad it had taken extreme measures for him to act like a worried parent.

"What the hell's going on? Why are we here?" Blaine asked. "Have they found Nathaniel? Did the police intervene in the negotiation?" He paled, turning his rage and concern on the police captain. "You gave me your word you would not interfere. What have you done? Haven't I given you enough? You were to stay out of this."

"I am." Caho scowled. "These men came to see me, not the other way around. I thought you were told to stay away from the police station."

Blaine turned his rage on Mercer. "Why are you involving the police?"

"Two members of my team are missing. They were in close proximity to a woman who worked for you. Your maid, to be exact. She was released with the other hostages. We happened upon her at a nearby pub. We believe she was targeted by the kidnappers, and I feared my team was wrongfully arrested for her murder. However, Captain Caho denies such claims."

"Do you have these men in custody?" Blaine asked.

"No, sir." Caho cowered.

Until now, Mercer was certain Caho wasn't working for the senator, but perhaps that was another lie.

"They better not be," Blaine said. "And nothing better happen to them either. Do I make myself clear?"

Caho nodded. "Perhaps your friends are looking for clues to this woman's murder. If we locate them, we will contact you." He gave Mercer a final look and retreated down the narrow hallway.

"Is that why you made me meet you here?" Blaine asked.

"I told you to wait outside." Mercer inhaled. "We should discuss the rest of these matters in private. My car is outside."

"So is mine," Blaine said. "What did the kidnapper say?"

"He wants to know if you've agreed to meet his demands."

"We need to return to my estate. The sooner, the better." Blaine gave the police station one last look. "Follow me."

TWENTY-TWO

"Jules," Hans whispered, "if Bas and Donovan aren't here, where are they?"

Mercer didn't break stride, but his mind twisted around the facts. At the door to the police station, he froze, failing to follow Blaine outside. "Stay with him. I'll be along shortly."

Hans continued out the door while Mercer spun on his heel. He squared his shoulders, bringing himself to his full height. At slightly over six feet with catlike reflexes and a build consistent with military special ops training, Mercer's presence could be quite intimidating. He eyed the inspector from across the room, gesturing that the man join him.

"Sir?" the inspector asked.

"I know the police questioned my men. Where are they?" He glared at the desk sergeant the second he reached for the telephone.

"I can't help you," the inspector said.

"You can, and you will." He'd dealt with hardened cops in the past, but this guy was nothing more than a rent-a-cop with a shiny gold shield. He didn't even have a real weapon, only a stun gun. "Where are they?"

Licking his lips, the inspector glanced down the hallway. "They're safe."

"Where?" Mercer's voice resonated from deep within his throat. The low snarl made the man step backward, fearing the deadly beast Mercer harbored within.

"Blaine's beach house."

Without another word, Mercer stormed toward the door. Stopping, he turned around, seeing the desk sergeant lift the phone. Briskly crossing the expanse, he yanked the receiver from the man's grip, ripped the entire phone free from its position on the desk, and tossed it in the trash receptacle on his way out the door. These morons had screwed with him one too many times. If they didn't get out of his way, he'd remove them permanently.

"Mr. Mercer," Blaine called from across the parking lot, "we don't have time to waste."

"Are you aware the police are at your estate? They have my men."

"Shit." Blaine glanced at his bodyguards. "Return to the hospital and stay with my wife." One of them opened his mouth to question the order, and Blaine shook his head. "Do what I say. I'm paying you enough. Now go." The man waiting in the passenger's seat of Blaine's sports car stepped out and joined his colleagues inside a black sedan. Once they pulled away, Blaine turned back to Mercer. "Let's go."

"Why are the police at your home?"

"I don't know."

Mercer's nostrils flared, but he kept his tone neutral. "How are you connected to the police?"

"I'm not." Blaine rubbed his eyes like he was weary.

"After you pulled me out of the car and they found Barbara in the trunk, they asked questions. I knew they were in Salvator's pocket, but I thought I could buy some time. Quite literally."

"Who's Salvator?"

"My associate. He threatened to put an end to this if I didn't."

"How?"

Blaine shrugged.

"Bollocks," Mercer swore.

"You paid Caho," Hans said. "What did you want him to do?"

"Nothing. I wanted him to keep his mouth shut about the situation and to stay out of the kidnapping. Wolf made it clear no one should get involved, that included the local police. We have to hurry. The longer we wait, the worse things will get. I'll answer whatever questions you have on the way, but please, let's go."

"It could be an ambush," Hans said. "Bas and Donovan might be bait."

"It isn't. The cops are looking for something. We should hurry before they find it," Blaine said.

Hans caught Mercer's eye, but he didn't speak. Instead, he held out his hand, and Mercer tossed him the car keys. Hans would be in the follow car. He'd run interference, check for tails, and provide additional protection should the senator's vehicle be stopped for any reason.

"By all means." Mercer gestured to the vehicle. "May I drive?"

Blaine climbed behind the wheel. "No one drives this baby but me. Get in."

Mercer kept his head on a swivel. "We searched your estate. I have the documents and account details from the hidden drawer in your son's dresser. What more do you have that can be exploited?"

"I have a list of contacts. I didn't divulge that intel to my partner, but since the police are searching my house, he must have heard about it." Blaine hit the gas, causing the wheels to spin. The man had no idea the proper way to control a car with this much power.

Mercer snorted at the irony. "Who knows about this list?"

"The private security company that temporarily replaced Darkfire. It's the list I gave them."

"Who else knows?"

"No one. Well, the kidnapper must since it was part of his ransom demand."

"You have a list of government assets hidden inside your home?"

"Yeah."

"Knob-end." Mercer flexed his fingers in an attempt to avoid hitting something, like the moron driving. "Was your wife aware?"

"No."

"Are you certain?"

"Why are you asking? What does she have to do with anything?"

"You sent guards to protect her as soon as you heard the police were at your home."

"So?"

"Has her health status changed?"

"The hospital hasn't phoned, so no."

"Then she's useless. They wouldn't have released her if she could have gotten them what they desire."

"How can you talk about her like that?" Blaine swerved over the yellow line. "Do you have any idea what it's like to be on the brink of losing someone you love?"

Mercer's already irritated demeanor soured further. "Do you?"

"Why do you think they took your men?"

Mercer remained silent, noticing Hans had closed the distance between them due to Blaine's erratic driving.

"How are we on time?" Blaine tried again. "You said Wolf wanted a response in an hour. Is he going to call back? Do you call him? How do these negotiations work?"

"We have time." Mercer had set the clock on his watch, and it was counting down. "He will phone again, expecting an answer. Once he receives it, a time and place will be determined."

"And then you just hand over everything, and he gives us Nathaniel? It's that easy?"

"It can be."

"What does that mean?"

"Wolf's unpredictable."

"Then make him predictable." Blaine turned to Mercer, once again letting the car veer too far to the side. "You must be able to do something. There has to be a way to control the situation. Isn't that your job? Isn't that what you do?" The angry, petulant tone was back. "You can't control him, can you?"

"No."

"That's why Barbara's in a coma and," he gripped the wheel, jerking it hard to the left and causing the rear to fishtail, "these assholes still have Nathaniel. Why did my insurance firm contact you? What makes you so damn special? Is this because of your connection to Wolf?"

"No. My team received the call because we were available and willing to assist. It is your connection to these alleged drug dealers that has created this problem. What demands did Wolf place on you, and how is it that you now plan to appease him? When last we spoke, you said that was impossible."

"Things change. I made some calls. People owe me favors. Other politicians owe me favors. My mistake will be considered an innocent indiscretion rather than treason. Luckily, I can make some things happen, but you'll have to act on my behalf for the delivery. That was one of Wolf's stipulations."

"I'm aware."

"Inside my estate are maps, plans, trade routes, names of individuals who control the most lucrative ventures in the war-torn portions of the Middle East. The person who possesses this information has the ability to take over and capitalize on the opportunities available. Wolf didn't find the intel when he was inside my home." Blaine smiled. "And from the look on your face, you and your men didn't come across it either. Or you did but didn't realize what you had."

"That's why the police are searching your estate." Mercer nodded at the two patrol cars parked at the front door. "And that's why they took Bastian and Donovan."

"My partner must have tipped off Caho. The police captain is in the pocket of the highest bidder. Salvator is getting nervous after the kidnapping and sent Caho to take control of any intel I possess to prevent me from delivering it. Unfortunately, my partner's pockets are deeper than mine."

"Your partner controls a cartel. He has infinitely more resources than you."

"I have the power of one of the strongest nations in the world backing me up. He can't say that. I'm pretty much bulletproof."

"You're not." For the briefest moment, Mercer wanted to disprove Blaine's statement, but he resisted. The last few days were evidence enough, but somehow, the senator had forgotten this. "Nothing can be done to save your son until my team is made whole again."

"Then get inside, get them together, and get this shit done. I'm not paying you to dick around and screw in my affairs if it doesn't get me what I want. You failed my wife. You will not fail me."

Mercer stepped out of the car and nodded to Hans who blocked the only exit. Bastian and Donovan better be unharmed or there would be hell to pay.

TWENTY-THREE

Mercer was acutely aware of Blaine's footfalls behind him, but he disregarded the senator's proximity as a threat. The real threat was somewhere inside the vast estate. Drawing his weapon, Mercer nudged the already opened front door with his shoulder and eased inside.

"Wait here," Mercer said.

Chatter came from the rear of the building. Mercer placed a finger to his lips to ensure Blaine would remain silent and edged forward, checking the rooms and doorways as he went. It was possible the police had brought other guests with them to search the property for the ransom. They couldn't be trusted. They had lied, allowed Wolf's associate to escape, and were here to do the cartel's bidding.

Stepping into the kitchen, Mercer spotted Donovan and Bastian seated at the table. Bastian was tinkering with the wiring of the microwave, and Donovan was working on unlatching a second set of handcuffs. At the sound of Mercer's footsteps, they looked up.

"It's bloody good to see you, mate." Bastian dropped the wires onto the table. His gaze shifted to the senator who hadn't listened to a single word Mercer had said. "Sorry for the mess. They insisted." He jerked his head toward the hallway. "Four bobbies, minimally armed, but those bloody zappers really screw with the nervous system."

"All right?" Mercer asked.

"Just the occasional twitch." Donovan unlatched the second set of handcuffs that bound his ankles to the chair leg.

"They forced us to help them search, but since we weren't the least bit helpful, they stuck us in here." Bastian looked at the mess he'd made. "I rigged this monitor and managed to flick on the internal cameras. We planned on getting out of here but thought it might be best to determine what they were after first."

"Any ideas?" Blaine asked.

"It doesn't matter. We already know what they want," Mercer said. "Don't we?"

The senator nodded. "We should stop them before this gets further out of hand."

"Jules," Bastian warned, "we haven't exactly been arrested, but leaving has been discouraged." He held up his wrist as if to demonstrate, but the handcuff dangled ineffectually. "Apparently, we weren't supposed to free ourselves. They did have us chained to the table for good measure. It was a feeble attempt at best, but we stuck around anyway. The more we humiliate the police, the more likely they are to retaliate."

"Caho's dirty, but that discussion can wait."

"I don't know that it can." Donovan looked uneasy. "Wolf's team murdered the woman. It was a clean kill. Headshot. Dead center."

"After that, they made a mess out of the rest of the bar," Bastian said. "They murdered her right there, and no one noticed. She slumped back in the chair. It was quiet. They had a silencer, and with the loud music, no one heard the pop. Donovan and I were the only ones near her. Her friends had already gone. No one would have known, which is why they shot up the rest of the bar with automatic fire. The shooter wanted the police to come. They wanted to jam us up. They might have planned all this just so the police could bring us here. Something big is going on."

"Shall we have a chat with the coppers? We can ask nicely, if you like," Donovan said.

"Donovan, with me. Once the threat has been neutralized, Bas will shadow the senator to retrieve whatever sensitive materials remain inside the estate." Spinning, Mercer faced the senator. "Stay here."

After handing Donovan his back-up weapon, Mercer went down the hallway. His previous visits made navigating the estate easier. They approached the doorway to the home theater room. Signaling to Donovan, Mercer entered low and remained hidden behind the couch. Donovan followed, taking up a position at the other end of the sofa.

Mercer moved behind one of the officers searching the large entertainment center. Each DVD case had been opened, checked, and tossed. The growing heap meant the police hadn't found anything, and Mercer wasn't sure they would.

"Gentlemen," he yanked the stun gun free from the officer's belt as Donovan snuck around and did the same to the second bobby, "I believe this is breaking and entering."

"How did you get free?" the cop asked.

"Easy, mate. Perhaps you'll be able to do the same." Donovan nodded down at the man's wrist which was now bound to the furniture.

"You're interfering in a kidnapping negotiation." Mercer flipped through the settings on the stun gun. "Who sent you?"

"We're just doing our job," the second cop answered.

Mercer pressed the taser against the man's neck, shocking him until he dropped to his knees. "Who sent you?"

"Captain Caho. We're here to help."

"That's doubtful."

Donovan smiled. "What precisely are you searching for? You wanted our help, but you were a bit vague." He looked at the stacks of discarded DVDs. "I don't think you're going to find a copy of *Police Academy*."

The bound cop scowled. "Screw you."

Donovan checked his taser. "I don't see that setting here. Let's go with this one instead." He gave the bound cop a jolt and glanced at Mercer. "I couldn't let you have all the fun." He turned back to the cop. "Want to try again? I have four more settings to test out."

"We were told to search everything. Something valuable is hidden here. If we can find it, we can help the senator get his son back," the cop explained. "We're just following the captain's orders."

"How did Caho get involved?" Mercer flipped the stun gun to max.

Both officers stared at Mercer like he had asked the dumbest question imaginable. "We questioned the released hostages, rescued Mrs. Blaine from the trunk of the car, and have been guarding Mr. Blaine ever since. This is our job."

"No. It's mine."

"Enough," Blaine said from the doorway. Bastian was right behind him with two other police officers in tow. "I've spoken to your captain. The police are not to be involved in my affairs." He focused on Donovan. "Uncuff him." Then he addressed the cops. "While I appreciate your assistance, a police presence threatens my son's life. I want you out of here immediately."

Mercer eyed Bastian, conveying the question, *Whose side is the senator on?*

Bastian cocked an eyebrow as if to say *who knows.*

Blaine stormed out of the room and down the hallway, leaving the K&R specialists with the four pissed off police officers. Grudgingly, Donovan uncuffed the bound man, and the two other officers helped their downed colleagues regain their footing.

"We'll clean up this mess and be on our way," one of them said.

"See that you are." Mercer led the way out of the room and took up a position at the end of the hallway to keep an eye on the police and await Blaine's return.

"This is rubbish. The police are working for the kidnapper. I don't care what they say. The Wolf Pack was waiting for us at the bar. They used the woman as bait. It's all part of their endgame. Unfortunately, I don't know what precisely that entails." Bastian rubbed a hand down his chin. "The police didn't even flinch at the body. They knew the woman would be executed. They knew we weren't responsible, just like they didn't waste their time running us down over the violence in the hotel. Either Wolf is controlling them, or whoever is controlling Wolf also owns the island's police force. They want this kept unofficial. No paper trail. No arrest records. They want to make sure nothing becomes official, including the reason why we're on this godforsaken island in the first place."

"Is Blaine safe alone?" Mercer asked more out of curiosity than actual concern. The senator hadn't listened to any of Mercer's instructions, and even now, he had gone off to retrieve the materials alone.

"I have no idea. The police had plenty of opportunities to harm him previously, so he should be fine." Lifting a small device, Bastian flicked to the camera which showed Blaine leaving the master suite and heading down the steps. After he returned to that floor, Blaine held up a finger, instructing Mercer and his team to wait while he entered the home theater room. "He's a bleeding idiot."

"No, he isn't. He knows more than what he's telling us." Mercer watched Blaine speak to the officers. "He acted like he had no interaction with Caho, but when push came to shove, he let slip that he paid the man. I don't know what side they're on. And we don't have time to figure it out."

Blaine sifted through the stacks of movies. Finally selecting one that hadn't been touched, he opened it, placed something inside his coat pocket, and replaced the box on the shelf.

"Did they ever give any indication what they hoped to find?" Mercer asked.

"They wanted our help to search, but they didn't tell us what to look for," Donovan said. "They were more interested in learning what we had already found."

"How did you know we were here? Did you come to spring us, Jules?" Bastian asked.

"More or less. Something's changed with our client. Suddenly, he's decided to give in to Wolf's demands. That's why we came here."

"So it's a lucky coincidence you stumbled upon us."

"No." Mercer's eyes flicked from Donovan to Bastian. "You were delayed. We came looking. It led to the bar. Someone from Wolf's team reported our reappearance, and Wolf phoned with an updated timetable. It's almost time for a call back. Where are your weapons?"

"Locked in the boot of the police car," Donovan said.

"Get them." Mercer checked the screen again, seeing Blaine headed toward the door. "Hans is monitoring the situation outside. With the traps Wolf has been setting, we need to get away from here as quickly as possible. The cops brought you here, and Wolf's demands lured Blaine back here. It's likely a trap. Wolf has us precisely where he wants us. If the police force is working for Wolf, like you suspect, he'll be notified as soon as we leave."

"Brilliant," Donovan muttered, leading the way to the front door with Bastian at his heels.

Mercer went down the hallway and grabbed Blaine. "Senator, let's go."

"Excuse me?"

"We have a deadline approaching. We came here with a purpose. You need to follow through."

"Sir," one of the officers said, "despite what you think, we're just trying to help."

"Then get out of our way." Mercer grabbed the senator's elbow and dragged him into the hallway. "Do you have the ransom?"

"Almost." Blaine tugged on the bottom of his jacket. "Keep them occupied. My secrets are none of their business or yours."

Blaine moved down the hallway and entered the laundry room. Mercer watched the officers closely. When one of them reached for his radio, Mercer lifted his gun and aimed at the man.

"Don't."

The cop held up his hands. "I was just going to say we were heading back."

"Did Wolf hire you? Or are you working for the

cartel?"

No one answered, but Mercer saw the recognition on their faces. The name meant something, which indicated Wolf had lined their pockets.

"Senator Blaine, it's time to go," Mercer called. He looked back at the men. "Tell Wolf he'll get what he wants, but if he touches a hair on that boy's head, he'll pay for it. And if I find out any of you were directly involved, you'll regret it."

Mercer put an arm around Blaine's shoulders and dragged the man out of the house, shushing him as he attempted to protest. The clock was ticking. Any second, the estate could turn into a deathtrap.

Nightfall provided limited cover, but it also meant Wolf and the other PMCs would have to use infrared or night vision to monitor the area. Mercer met up with Bastian and Donovan in the front foyer.

"All set?" Mercer asked, and they nodded. "Senator, we have every reason to believe we were lured here this evening. In the event this is a trap, it'd be best if you come with us. We can offer you protection."

"I have my own protection. I'm in possession of the ransom. Need I remind you of the type of protection you afforded me and my wife?"

"Fine. I will accompany you."

"No need."

"Sir, I must insist." Mercer stepped closer, but Blaine held up his hand.

"I trust you will speak to the kidnapper when he phones again. Tell him I have the materials he needs. Then set up the exchange. I'll be with my wife if you need me, and I would like some privacy." He walked out without another word.

"Senator," Mercer cautioned but stopped after one word. There was no reason to waste his breath on deaf ears.

"Jules, let's get this show on the road," Bastian urged, edgier than usual. "We'll follow and keep him in our sights."

Nodding, Mercer removed the torch from his pocket and signaled to Hans, who drove to the front door to minimize the risk of being picked off by sniper fire on the way back to the car. Once inside the vehicle, Mercer instructed Hans to follow the senator, who was now barreling down the driveway at top speed. Even if the nutcase didn't deserve their protection, he had within his possession the ransom that would free the boy. That was something worth protecting.

The vehicles had just cleared the guard station and turned onto the main road when a loud pop sounded. The senator's sports car swerved hard to the right. The sudden shift in velocity caused it to career onto its side and collide with a tree.

Hans slammed on the brakes.

"Close the distance," Mercer barked at the exact instant automatic fire punched into the side of their vehicle. "It's an ambush."

TWENTY-FOUR

Insisting on armored vehicles was one of the few constants in Julian Mercer's life. The bullets continued to impact, but they had yet to pierce the outer shell of the SUV. Several more shots came from another direction, hitting the rear and corner panel. From their current position, they couldn't determine the senator's condition.

Blaine's car was sideways, the hood crushed and mangled against what remained of a palm tree. Fluids leaked, causing a reflective sheen on the roadway. The smell of burnt rubber and petrol filled the air. If the men firing weren't careful, they would ignite the car and destroy every shred of hope they had of obtaining the ransom. No movement came from inside the senator's sports car. Blaine could be unconscious or dead.

"Use our vehicle as a shield." Mercer checked his handgun. "Donovan, there's a rifle in the back."

"Got it." Donovan loaded the gun and pocketed a handful of rounds. "What's the play?"

"Jules," Bastian warned, "we can't get Blaine out of there. We're pinned from both sides. One step out of this SUV is suicide." He chambered a round and tucked an extra magazine into his pocket. "I thought they didn't want to kill him."

"They don't need him anymore. He has the ransom. That's all they want, and if they get it, he serves no purpose, just like his son." Mercer spotted a tear in the soft top of the convertible. "We have to save the ransom."

"We should save his sorry arse while we're at it." Hans kept one hand on the steering wheel while the other aimed in the direction of the incoming barrage. "I can lay down cover fire, but you'll have to be quick."

"Donovan, is there any spare petrol?" Mercer asked, a plan formulating in his mind.

Donovan passed him the container. The red canister didn't possess much heft. The emergency fuel had been placed in the boot when the team rented the vehicle, but it wasn't something they had bothered to inspect.

"This will have to do," Mercer said. "Bas, I need your lighter."

"Don't blow us all to kingdom come." Bastian handed over the Zippo.

"There's not enough petrol for that, but they don't know it." Mercer reached for the door handle, and Bastian grabbed his shoulder.

"I'm coming with you." Shifting places with Donovan, Bastian brought his weapon to the ready. "Someone has to hold them off while you bluff our way out of this predicament." He paused for half a second. "You are bluffing, right, Jules?"

Mercer didn't answer. Instead, he unlocked the door and slid out, closing it as quickly as possible and ducking down. Bastian appeared at his side, aiming into the darkness at the rear of the vehicle. A few shots flew toward them, and Bastian returned fire. From the other side of the vehicle, sounds of Hans' handgun boomed, meeting the echoing call of enemy gunfire. Another volley of shots came from the side.

"We're surrounded." Donovan rolled down the rear window, climbed to his knees, and steadied the long gun by placing the barrel through the narrow opening. "I'm switching sights." He readjusted the weapon, cycling through his options until he found a night vision scope. "Two men directly in front of us, roughly fifty meters." He fired. "Bogey down. Repositioning."

Before he could fire again, projectiles blasted toward them from all sides. Bastian flattened onto the ground beside Mercer. The sound of bullets colliding with the armored vehicle grew louder and more frequent. Eventually, the pockmarks would become holes, or the bullet-resistant glass would shatter. Waiting for the other side to run out of ammunition was a foolish endeavor. Mercer signaled to Bastian, and they army-crawled toward the sideways sports car.

"Any farther and we're in the open. We'll be sitting ducks. Whatever you're planning on doing, I suggest you do it now," Bas said.

Mercer lifted himself to his knees. "Lay down suppressive fire." He removed the cap on the petrol can, stood, and heaved it onto the senator's wreck. He flicked the lighter and held the flame over the leaked fluids. "Don't shoot or Blaine and the ransom go up in flames." His voice carried through the dark and wooded area. Hopefully, the enemy was paying attention.

Several shots hit the side of the SUV, several centimeters from Mercer. However, the implied threat did not force Julian to back down. He took a step closer to the sideways sports car, never letting the flame of the lighter go out.

"You wouldn't harm Blaine. You're here to protect him," a disembodied voice shouted.

"I'll kill him and destroy the ransom before I let you take it. Is that clear?" Mercer knew these men would do anything to get their hands on that ransom. Another wayward shot whizzed past his head, closer this time. "You better make sure I don't drop this, or everything goes up in a blaze." He stepped closer to the wrecked vehicle and held the lighter over the driver's door where the empty petrol can remained. Spinning around, he shouted to whoever was listening, "You missed. You want to give it another go?"

"Jules," Bastian said, "stop being bloody suicidal." Inching forward on his belly, he muttered a few prayers and curses. "I'll get the senator." He remained crouched while slicing through the top of the sports car.

"Hurry," Mercer said.

Once the soft top was torn asunder, Bastian pulled it free, finding a dazed and terrified Blaine hugging the steering wheel. "Sir, are you sure you don't want to ride with us?"

Blaine was disoriented. A deep laceration ran from his scalp down his jaw. His eyes weren't focused, but he was ambulatory. "He's crazy. He plans to cook me alive."

"He still might," Bastian replied. "We need to hurry. Do you have the ransom?"

"Yeah," Blaine patted his jacket pocket, feeling the reassuring heft, "but I can't get out. My leg's stuck under the steering column."

More shots were fired in their direction. One struck the front end of the sports car, producing a high-pitched metallic ding that reverberated throughout the vehicle. Blaine cringed, curling into a compromised fetal position.

"Buy us some time, Jules." Bastian slid deeper into the car just as another shot rang out, narrowly missing his thigh. "I'm not sure they believe you."

"Idiotic sods." Mercer aimed in the direction of the last shot fired. Squeezing off three rounds, he waited, but there was a delay in the return fire. Maybe these morons had gotten smarter in the last few minutes.

"Commander," Donovan said just loud enough for Mercer to hear, "we have movement. I'm picking up three bogeys at two o'clock. They might have reinforcements. I think they plan to box us in."

"Do what you can."

Hans and Donovan opened fire. Donovan focused on the congregating group of combatants while Hans fired into the wooded area adjacent to the driver's side of the car. After emptying their magazines, silence ensued. No one else fired, but Mercer wasn't optimistic enough to believe the threat was neutralized. Perhaps the enemy had sought cover or were planning a retaliatory strike.

"How's it coming along?" Mercer whispered.

"I've got him. We're ready to come out. We might need a diversion," Bastian said.

In the darkness, Mercer smiled. "Get out of there now." Lifting his handgun, he fired a spread, spanning the entire one hundred and eighty degrees in front of him. He squeezed the trigger a final time, and the gun clicked empty. "Things are about to heat up. Move out."

As soon as Bastian wriggled free from the decimated roof, dragging Blaine behind him, Mercer dropped the lighter on top of the vehicle. The sudden flare-up temporarily blinded anyone using night vision or infrared and provided the three men enough time to get into the SUV.

A millisecond after the door slammed shut, another round of fire bombarded the armored truck, this time cracking the windshield, the rear window, and leaving several deep pockmarks in the metal.

"We need to get out of here." Hans dropped his weapon to his lap and knocked the SUV into reverse. Peeling away from the emblazoned sports car, he placed his hand on the back of the passenger's seat and drove backward. Once the incoming bullets were only being fired into the front of the SUV, Hans whipped the vehicle around and drove at breakneck speed away from the ambush. "Everyone good?"

"Good?" Blaine balked.

"Senator, hold still." Bastian leaned the man against the back of the seat while he assessed his injuries. "You might have a concussion."

"Let me see the intel." Mercer reached a hand behind him.

Before Blaine could voice a protest, Donovan removed a thick stack of folded papers, a disk, and an external hard drive from the senator's pocket.

"Where's your security?" Mercer asked. "Why aren't they here?"

"They are with my wife," Blaine said. "I didn't expect to need security at my own home while under your protection." He winced when Bastian pressed a clean cloth against the laceration on his face. "This is your fault. You said you were going to kill me. You let them do this to me. You knew they'd be there. You lured me here. You're working with them. You let them hurt Barbara." He blinked back the first sign of true remorse for his wife since she was pulled out of the back of the Land Rover. "It's been you this entire time." He shook his head, irate. "You have it now. You got what you wanted, so go ahead." He set his jaw and stared defiantly at Bastian and Donovan. "Kill me. It makes no difference anymore. I'm done."

"Stop acting like such a nutter," Donovan said. "We're here to help you. By the looks of it, we're the only ones willing to try."

"We need to switch vehicles and take him to the hospital," Mercer said, distracted by the confiscated intel. "We'll need to fully vet his security detail, and I think it's time the senator and his wife get off this island."

"I don't know if she's in any condition to be moved," Hans said.

"If she isn't, we'll have to find reliable protection for her." Mercer turned around in the seat so he could face Blaine. "After seeing this, it's no wonder they want you dead."

"Who do you think the shooters were?" Hans asked. "I thought the Wolf Pack was a six man team."

Mercer looked expectantly at Blaine. "Answer him."

"I don't know."

"I have a feeling your cartel connection has decided you're more trouble than you're worth," Bastian said. "You better hope Salvator hasn't struck a deal with the kidnappers."

TWENTY-FIVE

"Jules, we can't stay here all night," Hans murmured. They were positioned in the hallway outside Mrs. Blaine's hospital room. Harry Blaine had an orbital fracture from the crash but nothing too serious. "At some point, we need to check on our friend."

Mercer nodded but otherwise didn't acknowledge Hans or the fact they had a man detained inside their safe house. As usual, he was too busy constructing conspiracy theory on top of conspiracy theory, each one more feasible than the last. No one could be trusted. From the documents in Blaine's possession, everyone had a reason to eliminate or control this man, even his own government.

"Thanks, love," Bastian cooed, providing a thousand-watt smile to the floor nurse. "You're a real lifesaver, in more ways than one."

She blushed.

Hans snorted. "I'm impressed."

"Sod off," Bastian said, rejoining his teammates. "We needed internet access and a terminal." He

G.K. Parks

chewed on the end of his pen while he flipped the pages he printed. "Photo verification seemed pertinent given the givens." He scanned the images again, eyeing the bodyguards stationed inside Barbara's room and on the couches in the waiting area. "Minus the possibility of extensive plastic surgery, I'd say they are who they claim to be."

"Can they be trusted?" Mercer asked.

"No criminal records. No money troubles. No obvious blackmailable offenses. They were provided to the senator via a security firm that's been thoroughly vetted by various government officials and agencies. They're about as clean as we're going to find."

"Fine." Mercer's gaze ran down the length of the drab hallway, narrowing in on the security cameras. "Did you create a backdoor to monitor the situation here?"

"Of course."

"Clone his phone. We need to know with whom he's in contact."

Bastian removed his own phone and searched his programs for the proper one.

"Donovan," Mercer waved the man over, "did you learn anything from the bodyguards?"

"They're to provide protection to the Blaines until such a time that official protection is available. In other words, once the senator is stateside, they'll be dismissed."

"Do they know what's going on?" Hans asked.

"They haven't got a clue. They're in the same boat we are."

Mercer looked at his phone. Any call to the command center would be rerouted to his cell. But Wolf hadn't called back, which meant he was responsible for the ambush. However, Mercer

- 183 -

couldn't shake the feeling the police officers inside the estate had tipped off Wolf as soon as the senator and the negotiators left the property. The possibility that Wolf was aligned with the cartel did not bode well.

"Did we miss the deadline?" Hans asked.

"I don't know. Any suggestions on how to proceed?"

The uncharacteristic question took the men aback. Mercer always had a plan, even if it was crazy or dangerous. Asking for suggestions worried them. Bastian ground the end of the pen into a flat piece of plastic between his molars, and Hans pretended to be fascinated by the monitors visible through the closed door to Barbara Blaine's room.

Donovan met Mercer's eyes. "They murdered that woman in front of us." He looked down at a smattering of red flecks on his shirt. "In the future, I would prefer some distance between us and the growing number of casualties." He tossed a glance over his shoulder and into the room. "It's possible another attempt will be made on the Blaines, but staying here won't save the child. I say we move out and let someone else handle their private security. We have another job to do, and being here isn't getting it done."

"I agree. Any objections?"

Bastian removed the pen from his mouth. "Normally, I'd say we have to protect the family, but leaving them is our best option, particularly when Blaine doesn't want us around."

"They'll be shoving off soon enough," Hans said. "I spoke to the medical staff. Barbara is stable enough to be transported to a different facility. The only question is if Blaine is willing to abandon his son."

"He did once. He'll do it again." Mercer opened the door and went into Barbara's room. Keeping his focus away from the comatose woman, he cleared his throat.

The senator turned. "What do you want now? Has Wolf made contact?"

"No, sir."

"Why not? He was supposed to have called nearly two hours ago. What's the holdup?"

"I suspect his team is scrambling after their failed attempt to take the ransom by force."

"Well, good. Shouldn't you be doing something?"

"My team will formulate a plan. However, it's in your best interest to take your wife and get off this island as soon as you can. Once you get to safety, you will call me. If the kidnapper attempts to make contact with you or any of your staff, you will contact me. In the meantime, we will retain possession of the ransom and comply with the kidnapper's demands in order to retrieve your son."

"How do I know you aren't working with them or plan to keep that information for yourself?" Most of Blaine's bravado and arrogance had fizzled on account of the painkillers. Now he was just angry and afraid.

"You don't, but if you want to survive, you will do as I say." With that, Mercer turned and walked out of the room.

"Hey," Blaine shouted, jogging to catch up, "you can't just walk away from me."

"There is nothing left to discuss."

"The hell there isn't. You said I needed to be close for the negotiation. Now you want me gone."

"The situation has changed. They have decided you are expendable." Mercer turned away, but Blaine grabbed his shoulder. "Remove your hand, or I will."

"Jules," Bastian said, "easy."

Blaine's glare rivaled that of Mercer's. "This is my life. These people came into my world and turned it on its head. Then you trot in and do the exact same thing. Should I remind you that you have done nothing to help? My wife is in that room," he pointed emphatically to the door behind him, "because of you and your failure to resolve this." He put air quotes around the word resolve, as if he'd heard Mercer say it one too many times to consider it believable. "I'm not going anywhere until my son is back in my arms, alive and well. Do I make myself clear?"

"Was he alive and well the last time you saw him?"

Blaine flushed a deep crimson and threw a punch. Mercer batted his arm away with ease. The man swung again with his left. Knowing this wouldn't stop until a hit connected, Mercer didn't bother to block. The physical sting was barely noticeable compared to the razor-sharp accusation.

"Don't even pretend you understand what I'm going through." Blaine scowled. "How am I supposed to trust you'll rescue him and return him unscathed?"

"Then feel free to hire someone else to solve your problems. Let's clear out." Mercer marched toward the exit, leaving an exasperated Blaine in his wake.

Once they were outside, Hans fell into step beside Mercer. "We have to save the boy."

Mercer snorted, knowing damn well he couldn't walk away from this any more than his team could. He just needed some distance from their insufferable client. It didn't matter if Blaine hired every negotiator on the planet. By the time any of them arrived, it'd be too late. Blood had been shed on their watch. They had to see it through to the end. Fuck Blaine's orders. He got his family into this mess, and only a professional could get them out of it.

"Julian, stop." Hans moved to block his path. "I'm not leaving."

"None of us are, mate," Bastian said from several meters away. "You ought to know the commander better than that." He tapped against the locked door. "Who the bloody hell has the keys to this thing?"

Before Hans could ask any questions, Blaine exited the hospital with two of his bodyguards.

"Mr. Mercer," Blaine said, "you know damn well I can't change horses midstream, particularly when you have the ransom in your possession. So I have no choice but to stick with you."

"Mr. Blaine, go inside. Standing out in the open isn't safe."

Blaine paled, becoming so white he was practically phosphorescent in the moonlight. "You think they'll try again?"

"Why wouldn't they?" Hans asked. "They wanted you dead a couple of hours ago. What have you done since to change their minds?"

Blaine stared at Mercer. "The first thing you need to do is negotiate the target off of me. Tell them if any other attempts are made, the deal's off." His good eye twitched. "I want this handled immediately. We will meet for breakfast to discuss everything else." He waved a dismissive hand in Mercer's face. "Go on."

Without so much as a word, Mercer removed the car keys from his pocket and unlocked the doors. "Mercurial twit."

"Fickle doesn't even begin to describe him." Bastian slid into the passenger's seat. "One minute, he fires us. The next, he rehires us."

"Puerile wanker," Donovan agreed.

"At least we have a consensus on our client," Hans said. "Now will someone please explain to me what is going on? We were nearly slaughtered trying to protect that pathetic prick, and for the life of me, I have no idea why."

"Wasn't it your idea to save him when we were pulling the ransom out of the wreckage?" Donovan grinned. "Perhaps you need to ask yourself some very important questions, like why you're such a bad judge of character."

Bastian turned to Mercer. "It's time you clue us in on the situation."

"Our first priority is contacting Wolf. He needs to know we have the ransom and are prepared to deliver. After that, we scramble." Mercer put the car in gear, glancing briefly at the cell phone he placed on the dash. No missed calls. Obviously, Wolf had decided to try to take what he wanted instead of barter for it. "The coppers can't be trusted. From now on, we tread lightly. Avoidance is recommended."

"What does Wolf want?" Bastian asked.

"Members of Darkfire traded excess American munitions for drugs. Despite the fact they were fighting insurgents, they were also supplying said insurgents with the weapons being used against their own. The drugs were then shipped worldwide in the cargo containers that once housed the weapons. They were divided up and distributed, possibly as payment in exchange for military or defense intelligence. The cartels didn't appreciate the competition, and one, in particular, put the screws to Blaine."

"Salvator, his not so silent partner?" Bastian asked, and Mercer nodded. "Bugger."

"How does this relate to Wolf and the kidnapping?" Donovan asked.

"Blaine was approached and pressured to withdraw the government contract from Darkfire, subsequently ending their stint in the opium trade and dissolving the government involvement in dealing arms and drugs for intelligence."

"Don't forget, Blaine sold out military operations and government assets when he handed over classified intel to some temporary private security groups during the transition," Bastian added. "And I'm fairly certain those private groups were legitimized facets of the cartel."

"Suffice it to say, Wolf and several other PMCs weren't pleased to lose a seven figure income. They want their money," Mercer said.

"That's why they want five million," Hans said.

"From the estimates in Blaine's ledger, the actual number is closer to fifty million."

"Shit." Hans rubbed a hand down his face. "How is that even possible?"

"Opium addiction is rampant. It's all about supply and demand," Bastian mused. "The U.S. government supplied the weapons cache to the PMCs to trade. Heavy artillery, grenades, SAMs, rifles. The list could go on forever. That gave them access to the opium and the poppy fields." Bastian glanced at Mercer to make sure he was on the right track. "Whatever resources the region has, the insurgents were willing to trade for weapons since the war's been waging for some time. Honestly, the entire region's been ravaged for decades. Terrorist cells pop up overnight. Some disappear almost as quickly, but they need equipment to fight. They'd be willing to do anything for it, including trading on the region's rich natural resources. It was easily exploitable."

"Yeah." Donovan shook his head, remembering a few of their grittier missions. "If they weren't attacking with AKs, they had M16s. Half the time, they were better equipped than we were."

"None of that matters," Mercer said.

"What do you mean it doesn't matter?" Donovan asked.

"We are here to negotiate the release of Nathaniel Blaine. He matters. Nothing else does."

"Jules," Bastian hedged, "we can't give them what

they want. Wolf wants intel to retake the region. It'll fuck with military operations of all allied nations, and it could cause a drastic shift in intelligence gathering and defensive measures. We don't possess that kind of knowledge. Does Blaine?"

"I don't know. He changed the tides once. They believe he can do it again."

"I'm guessing the bloke we tied up can shed some light on things. It'll be nice to have some sound questions to ask this time," Hans said. "No wonder we have American spies shitting themselves to get these details. Shouldn't they have had eyes on Blaine the entire time? Why did they let the kidnapping happen?"

"How do we know they aren't behind it?" Mercer asked.

"You mean the tosser with the camera?" Donovan snorted. "I knew he wasn't just some bloke with a weird fetish."

TWENTY-SIX

Before they even stepped foot inside the flat, Mercer drew his weapon. Signaling for Donovan and Hans to go around, he went to the door with Bastian at his six. The lock remained in place, but the tiny bits of crushed glass on the doorstep indicated someone had been here and left. Bastian scanned the doorframe for signs of a tripwire, but he didn't spot one. Mercer removed the keys from his pocket and unlocked the door. Holding his breath, he turned the knob and gently pushed it forward a centimeter at a time.

Bastian leaned in, checking for signs of a trap. "Clear," he whispered.

Opening the door wider, Mercer eased inside, going in high and to the left while Bastian went in low and to the right. Nothing had been touched. After meeting at the rear door, the team split up. Donovan turned down the hallway, assisting Bastian in checking the other rooms, while Mercer and Hans approached the cupboard where they'd locked up their captive.

"He's gone." Hans lowered his weapon. "Bugger."

The tape had been sliced, and the handcuffs were left on the seat of the chair, along with the hood and headphones. "How did he get free?"

"His people came for him. Our location's been compromised. We've been compromised. They had us the moment we turned that phone on."

"Jules, I believe this was meant for you." Donovan handed Mercer a sheet of paper.

Go to the fish market at two p.m. if you want answers.

"What's going on?" Bastian read the note. "Shall we start packing?"

Mercer looked at the time. He needed to make contact with Wolf. They had several meetings planned for the morning, which was in a couple of hours, and making another move would cost them precious time they didn't have.

"Do a thorough sweep for bugs. Run diagnostics on our equipment. At the present, assume everything is compromised." Mercer studied the photo array on the wall. Something was odd about their maps. Several new circles had been drawn. A few were in the waters surrounding the island, and three were at various points on the island. Picking up the stack of dossiers, Mercer flipped through the profiles on Wolf's team. A new one had been added for the senator's maid, a.k.a. Jezebel. She was trained by the Israeli army, moved to Europe, and suspected of providing anti-terrorist intel to the Mossad before becoming a soldier of fortune. She was wanted for crimes in several countries under an assortment of aliases. "Check everything." He held up the newest additions that had materialized. "Start with the phones."

Bastian retrieved his gear and scanned for listening devices. Since the flat was suspect, Mercer returned to the SUV and called Wolf.

"Did I miss your call?" Mercer asked.

"No," Wolf said. "Tell me something. Would you have really set that bastard on fire?"

"If it proved necessary."

"And they say I'm cold-hearted. I assume you have the ransom."

"Yes, but there are new conditions."

"You do not specify conditions. I have the boy. I am in control. Do you want me to send his lifeless body back to his father to prove my point?"

"No, but I want a new proof of life video sent to my phone immediately. Once that's done, we can move forward. I have what you want. Senator Blaine has willingly agreed to meet your demands as long as you do not make another attempt on his life or harm his son. Is that understood?"

"What if I don't agree? What are you going to do then?"

"This negotiation will cease. The ransom will forever be out of your reach. How badly do you want it?"

"How badly do you?"

Mercer's phone beeped, and he held it away from his face, opening the video file. The boy was shackled to the end of a metal cot, facing away from the camera. From what Mercer could see, he was breathing, likely sobbing, but there was no audio. The timestamp on the video said it had just been taken, but it could have been doctored or altered. However, drawing the veracity of the video into question wasn't a smart move.

"We can proceed," Mercer said, pressing the phone to his ear. "How quickly can we make the exchange?"

"You have everything?" Wolf asked, an air of unbelieving in his tone. "It's amazing how quickly things can be collected with a bit of incentive, isn't it?

When I wanted an audience with the senator, he was too busy. For months, I was neglected, denied access, denied the decency of an e-mail or a phone conversation, and now, well, look at things now. It's amazing how shit changes when a few people get killed. I guess I was wrong, and Blaine doesn't want his son dead after all. You'd never know he gave a shit about the kid from the way he acted at all those family outings and picnics. Surprise, surprise. Fine. Have everything ready to go. I'll give you a call when you should deliver. It's about time the senator waits around for someone to get back to him."

"Let's discuss some of the details now. I want to be prepared."

"I'll let you know what I decide. Be ready to move when I say so." Without another word, Wolf hung up.

Mercer watched the video another three times before returning inside. He'd need Bastian to parse it for extraneous details that might provide a location. That would be their next focus, followed by examining whatever data was contained on the disk and external hard drive that made up a large portion of the ransom demand. They had five hours until dawn. If only there was a way to make time stand still.

"Are we clear?" Mercer asked, stepping inside to find Bastian seated behind his laptop.

"No obvious eavesdroppers, but who knows." Bastian clicked a few more keys. "They copied our files. Everything we have, they have. I'm checking for malware, worms, and trojans. I don't like this. Who did this?"

"We were hoping you could tell us," Hans said. "Jules phoned that FBI lady for help, but her clearance level wasn't high enough."

Bastian swiveled, meeting Mercer's eyes. "You rang Parker? Did she at least verify these bastards are U.S.

agents?"

"Former military, the file has been redacted, but we know the cameraman is currently active in some sort of government capacity."

"A spook." Bastian shifted his attention back to the computer. "No wonder they did a decent job bypassing my system's security without frying the damn thing. I'll give 'em props. What's his name?"

"Alexander Loren." Hans opened one of the weapon cases and checked for signs of tampering. "Are we meeting him at two p.m.?"

"I'll run a background and see what I can get on his mission details. I'm starting to think every player is some form of American soldier," Bastian said, "but meeting with an ally can't hurt."

"It might." Hans closed one case and opened another, noticing Donovan doing the same. "This was the bloke responsible for getting Donnie knocked out cold, so we took some liberties. This wanker deserved it though. Nearly knocked my own block off with a broken chair. So I returned the favor and broke his arm."

"Great." Bastian sighed. "Anything else we should know?"

"He warned us the woman, the maid, that you and Donovan questioned, was working for Wolf." Hans held up the newest dossier their "allies" had left. "Believing you could be in peril, we came looking."

"Which is how Loren escaped," Mercer said.

"He must have known his people would come for him once they pinged his phone." Hans shook his head. "Stupid, stupid move. I should have never turned it on."

"We're desperate," Donovan said. "They know it. Everyone knows it. Wolf, these Americans, the local police, the cartel. They all do. We're surrounded on all sides. They're just waiting for a moment of weakness to move in and take what they want."

"They had to make sure we had it first." Mercer scooted the materials closer to Bastian. "After what transpired tonight, they know. They'll be coming for it if we don't end this quickly." He reloaded his weapon and placed a few extra magazines in his pocket. "Did you learn anything relevant from the woman before she was killed?"

"Based on what you've just said, it might have all been lies." Bastian's fingers danced over the keyboard as he attempted to break the encryption on the external hard drive.

Mercer looked at Donovan, who wasn't nearly as distracted. "Who killed her?"

"A sniper. I assumed one of Wolf's men, perhaps Fox or Hawke, but there's no way to know. They wanted to silence her. The police released her from custody just to throw her to the wolves."

"Quite literally," Hans retorted.

"She had us convinced she was a pawn in the game. She spoke of five masked men who broke into the house through the sliding glass door at the rear. The first two wore wetsuits. Once the security guard was neutralized and the system deactivated, the others arrived. They separated the staff, kept them downstairs in the dining room for a bit, tossed them into the maid's quarters, and eventually hauled them into the living room. After two days of being denied food, water, and sleep, they were marched outside. She thought it was going to be a mass execution. They were instructed to keep their mouths shut and not speak of it to anyone. The men knew everything about them. If any of them spoke, the gunmen would find out and do to their loved ones what they were planning on doing to the senator and his family. Then the men started shooting, and the lot jumped into the water. We know the rest." Donovan closed the weapon case.

"What about the police?" Mercer asked.

"She feared they had their own agenda and wanted to keep the hostages detained. The islanders know the police serve the cartel. Caho wanted to know about the ransom and the kidnappers, so they questioned everyone. But no one spoke. They were told they were being held in police custody for their own protection, but when a few of the senator's staff started squawking about their rights as U.S. citizens, the consulate was contacted. When they were picked up, the estate staff was free to go." Donovan shrugged. "We didn't get to ask about the other native staffers before she was killed. She didn't seem afraid when she spoke to us. She didn't seem flustered or anxious."

"Or traumatized," Bastian added. "I thought it was liquid courage, but she was just playing her part."

"She didn't count on Wolf wanting to keep a lid on things," Donovan surmised.

"You're assuming Wolf murdered her. It could have been the Americans or the cartel. All we know is the police expected to recover a body," Hans said.

"This is irrelevant. Did she say anything that would indicate where Wolf is holding the boy?" Mercer removed his phone and replayed the video.

"No." Donovan looked at the new circles on the map. "Do you think the Americans are trying to clue us in?"

"Or they want us to chase wild fowl," Bastian said. "I'm having problems getting into the hard drive. Even if I break the encryption, I can't guarantee they aren't monitoring my computer remotely. Do we want the Americans to know what we have?"

"Wasn't it theirs in the first place?" Donovan asked.

"I suppose." Bastian looked to Mercer for approval.

"Keep working. They know where we are and what we have. If they want it, they'll come for it. But first, we need assurances this is current. If the boy's dead, none of it matters."

After downloading the file, Bastian watched the video, checking for signs it had been doctored. "It appears genuine."

"At least we know he's alive." Hans sounded relieved. "Too bad we don't know where he is."

"The footage is stable, no pitch, no roll." Bastian picked up the closest pen and gnawed on the end. "I'd wager they're on land." His eyes shifted to the maps, which Donovan was examining. "Maybe our friendly neighborhood spy is on to something."

"I can run recon," Donovan offered. "We have a couple hours of nightfall remaining."

"Too many unknowns," Mercer said, but he considered the possibility of a preemptive sneak attack. "We'd have one shot, and if we screw it up, Nathaniel will be killed."

"Then what can we do?" Hans asked.

"We need to narrow the possibilities. The two of you, get whatever you can on the police officers who were inside Blaine's estate this evening. Those bastards made the call that signaled the ambush. Let's find out if they're double-dipping."

"It might be triple-dipping," Bastian said. "The cartel, the Wolf Pack, and Senator Blaine."

"Go. Watch yourselves," Mercer said, "but stay away from Caho. He's mine."

Hans and Donovan grabbed their gear and left without another word.

Once they were gone, Mercer picked up the files on the table. He had a few hours to reread every word and check for any discrepancies in what they previously possessed. Then he'd have to prepare for his meeting at the consulate and a debrief with Blaine. That was assuming Wolf didn't throw a wrench in their plans and request an immediate exchange and the Americans didn't raid the flat, take what they want, and kill the former SAS.

"These missions used to be simple."

"Nothing with you is ever simple, Jules." Bastian snorted. "But the shit must have really hit the fan for you to call Parker for a favor. Did you send her my love?"

"We'll discuss that later."

"You bet your arse we will."

TWENTY-SEVEN

"Time's up." Bastian watched Mercer press his palms into his eyes. "Do you want company for your meeting at the consulate?"

"No." Mercer put the maps and files down. He'd spent his time collecting as much data on the circled locations and updated dossiers as possible. What he needed most was access to Theodore Lamb, a.k.a. the Butcher. Being able to question that sadistic son of a bitch would provide the team with precious knowledge and possibly Nathaniel Blaine's location.

"You have just enough time to shower and change. I'll join you at the meeting with Blaine. I can't break the encryption on the hard drive, but it's probably worthless to us. The disk contains a spreadsheet of the value and quantity of the commodities being traded and the individuals providing intel or services in exchange. It's a hodgepodge of who's who of illicit dealings, but none of it will get us any closer to rescuing the boy. Perhaps speaking to the senator will shed some light on developing a recovery plan."

"Brilliant." Mercer headed into the bedroom. "You don't believe paying the ransom will result in a positive outcome?"

"Jules, handing this over is a bad idea."

"A drug cartel already possesses it and is exploiting it at this very moment, isn't that bad enough? We're not traitors like that pisser Blaine. This isn't our fight. How much worse could it get if we give it to Wolf? Didn't he and his people have it originally?"

"One would think. But Blaine told us he changed things. If these trade routes and contacts had been utilized by the PMCs, Wolf wouldn't be asking for this. Something else is going on. Since a clandestine government agency is monitoring Blaine's actions, they know what he's done and intend to remedy the situation. Shit, they might be the only ones who know the truth."

"Or they're here to kill him."

Mercer closed the bathroom door. Exhaling slowly, he stripped out of his clothes, catching a glimpse of the plethora of scars littering his torso. They'd been in some fine scrapes because of compromised intelligence, but there wasn't a doubt in his mind Blaine's actions had cost lives. Someone needed to fix things. Mercer possessed the information that could reestablish a balance or lead to further instability within a volatile region. Perhaps Bastian was right, and they couldn't hand this over to Wolf.

By the time he stepped out of the shower, dressed and ready to go, Donovan and Hans had returned from their outing. "The police are in the cartel's pocket," Donovan said. "They turn a blind eye to the island's drug trade. They don't arrest dealers or traffickers. They allow shipments to dock and leave without inspections. However, I assume that's the norm."

"Meaning?" Mercer armed himself with a few metal detector friendly items, just to be on the safe side.

"They're easily bought. We scouted some of their homes. Every single officer lives like royalty. From what we gather, when Wolf arrived, he paid them to look the other way. But the more we buggered about, the greater the need to keep tabs on us," Hans said.

"Do you have proof?" Bastian asked.

Hans smirked. "Let's just say we found a weak link."

"Did you do anything that would compromise our situation further?" Mercer asked.

"No, mate." Donovan shook his head. "We asked some polite questions, then we gave the copper a little something to put him out for the next eighteen hours and covered him in rum to make it appear to be a wicked hangover. There's not much chance he'll remember we spoke."

"Fine." Mercer looked at Bastian. "Set a clock. We'll have to be prepared to monitor him as well." He threw a glance at Donovan and Hans. "Don't muck about while I'm gone."

*　　*　　*

"Mr. Mercer," Jeremy Crawford, the consulate's talking piece, gestured to a chair at the conference table, "I'm sorry for the delay. I've been briefed on the situation concerning Senator Blaine. It's such a shame to hear the senator's family was targeted. As you know, his entourage was removed from police custody and brought here."

"All of them?"

"Those that we have jurisdiction over. We can only provide assistance to our citizens. I hear the senator hired several locals to serve as caretakers. It's my understanding they were sent home."

"I need to speak to Theodore Lamb."

Crawford's lips twitched. "I'm sorry, sir, but that won't be possible. As I was about to say, we thought it prudent to act swiftly once we became aware of the circumstances."

"Meaning?" The consulate was small. Based on size and dimensions, there weren't many places the staff could be housed. Mercer would be able to find them in a matter of minutes, but it would result in an international incident, and the guards with automatic rifles wouldn't take kindly to a frontal assault.

"We've had issues trusting the police in the past. They have an interesting way of approaching what we would consider law and order. The fact they were detaining victims against their will without cause or even an open investigation into the kidnapping makes us draw a lot of things into question. As it stands, the state department has issued a notice to warn travelers to use caution when visiting the island."

Giving the man his best *I don't give a shit* look, Mercer counted to five. "I need to speak to Lamb."

"I'm sorry. He was not brought to the consulate."

"He's working with the kidnappers. It is imperative I question him. Do you know where he is?"

"He's not here."

"Let me speak to the others."

"We booked return passage for the victims. The flight left four hours ago."

"Have they landed? Lamb needs to be detained. He's dangerous. We need to find him."

"Sir," Crawford hesitated, "we're not entirely positive the police aren't involved in his disappearance."

"Nitwits." Mercer went to the door, spotting the guard outside. "If you want to help, let me speak to

Alexander Loren."

"Who?"

Mercer studied the man, unsure if it was an act or if he honestly had no idea who Loren was. "Never mind. This was a waste of time. Just make sure you aren't so careless when it comes to booking safe passage for Blaine and his wife." Opening the door, he said to the guard, "I'm ready to leave."

"Please show Mr. Mercer out," Crawford said, "and godspeed. I hope you are able to save the boy."

TWENTY-EIGHT

Mercer stepped into Blaine's hotel room and glared at the bodyguards. Bastian hadn't arrived yet, which meant he had a few moments to get to the bottom of things. "I want the bloody truth, and I want it now."

"What are you bitching about?" Blaine asked. "What nonsense did the kidnapper fill your head with this time?"

"Your story doesn't make sense." Mercer went to the window, peering outside for signs of a sniper scope or enemy movement in the distance. To be on the safe side, he pulled the drape closed, wondering why the bodyguards hadn't insisted on that in the first place. "Lying to us is pointless. It hurts our chances of a positive recovery."

"Positive recovery, positive recovery. That's all I hear from you. Just call it what it is—the chance of getting my son back alive."

"Fine. Tell me the truth. You said you made a lucrative deal, handed over sensitive, classified materials to a drug kingpin, and now the PMCs who you put out of work want that intel. But if they had it in the first place, like you insist, why would they want it now?"

"They did have it, but the ransom isn't just about the classified intel. It's about the cartel's drug lines. Wolf wants the names of the farmers, the weapons dealers, and the places where these exchanges occur. That's what's lucrative. That's what he's after."

"And your kingpin associate, Salvator, will murder you because of it. But you aren't concerned about that. Instead, you fear being accused of treason, losing your seat in the Senate, and what your government might do to you. You talked about being paid off for your vote and those details coming to light, but it doesn't coalesce. Your story is rubbish."

"No, it isn't. I told you the truth. Every detail is what happened."

"This isn't Nicaragua. Don't tell me this is some modern-day Contra scandal."

"Of course it isn't. The U.S. government would never officially be part of something like that."

"But PMCs would?"

"Yes."

"Is Wolf working for the cartel?"

"I can't be sure." Blaine turned to the bodyguards. "You've heard enough. Leave us." The two men went into the adjacent room and closed the door. "I thought they were separate entities, but when you started asking questions about the cartel and how I ended up being lured to the island, things stopped making sense. The enemy of my enemy, right? The cartel stopped being an ally as soon as I realized my mistake when I handed over classified mission details to those private groups. I only learned of who they actually were after that. Before, I believed they were another security venture group that wanted a taste of action in the Middle East. I attempted to sever ties, but that made my associate leery."

"He sought out Wolf?"

"It was no secret Darkfire was pissed about losing the contract. Several of their men became very vocal, even threatening. Wolf was the loudest and most disgruntled. Salvator must have offered him a wonderful opportunity to scare the shit out of me and keep me in line," Blaine admitted. "Wolf and his men took over my entire estate. They shot some staff members. They beat my wife. Suffocated us. Tortured us. And they still have my son. All because of greed. My greed. Their greed. It's ridiculous." His eyes found Mercer's. "All the money in the world can't fix this, and that's all I cared about before any of this happened."

"You should have realized it sooner." Mercer wanted to know if Blaine was aware American agents were monitoring him, but asking would tip off the senator and might not serve any real purpose other than to spook the man. "Did you pay the police?"

"I tried. When they rescued me, I met with Captain Caho. I paid him several thousand dollars to look the other way and not open an official investigation. Wolf had been adamant about that, but Caho said you and your team had caused problems. He extorted twenty grand from me to turn a blind eye to your indiscretions." Blaine snorted. "You're welcome."

"Those alleged crimes were planted." Mercer shook his head. "No matter."

"Why do you ask?"

"The police are owned by the cartel. The officers at your estate tipped off the men who ambushed us. As of yet, we haven't determined if the shooters were part of the kidnapper's team or the cartel's."

"Didn't you just say they are one and the same?"

"So it would seem."

A knock sounded, and the two bodyguards from the other room emerged, weapons at the ready as they approached the door. Mercer's hand traveled to his holster, but he didn't clear leather. He knew who was knocking.

"You started without me?" Bastian pushed past the guards. "Are there any muffins? I thought this was a breakfast meeting. I'll take a spot of tea or some coffee if that's all that's left."

"Bas, stop focusing on your stomach."

"Fine." Bastian nodded to Blaine. "Good to see you are well, Senator. Sorry to crash your meeting, but I have some questions to ask." He pulled the external hard drive from his pocket and laid it on the table. "What is on this bloody thing, and how do I break the encryption?"

Blaine dropped into a chair, seemingly spent from the ordeal. "That's not important."

Bastian disagreed. "You said this was part of the ransom demand, so it must be valuable. What is it?"

"That isn't something you need to focus on. Your job is to negotiate an exchange and bring my son home. That's it. It ends there."

"With all due respect," Bastian said, "our actions have always been focused on rescuing your son. So when we ask a question, there's a reason. What's on the drive?"

"Leave it be. It's secure and encrypted. It won't do anyone any good. Not you. Not those sons of bitches who did this to my family or the cartel that manipulated me and my vote."

"Your own greed manipulated you. Answer the question." Mercer's eyes grew cold. "We won't trade it for your son unless you tell us what's on it."

"You can't do that."

"Hate to break it to you, mate, but we can do whatever we want." Bastian settled into one of the chairs, picked up the nearest mug, gave it a sniff, wiped the rim, and took a sip. "And I'd like some muffins while you're at it. Maybe a side of eggs and some of those bacon strips, extra crispy. Jules, would you like anything?"

"No." Amused, Mercer steepled his fingers, pressing them against his lips while he watched Bas go from good cop to bad cop. Days of sleep deprivation and stress had taken a toll, effectively breaking down Bastian's friendly, compassionate demeanor.

Taking a seat on the sofa, he had no issue letting this play out. Bas would get the information they needed. He always could.

Blaine opened his mouth to speak, but Bastian jerked his chin at the hotel phone.

"Room service will deliver. The placard says they serve breakfast for another thirty minutes. Best you hurry." Smiling brightly, Bastian opened his computer bag and removed the laptop. "Don't dawdle." He nudged his chin at the phone again while he removed a few accessories and turned on the device.

"Senator, if you'd be so kind." Mercer stifled a laugh.

After the breakfast order was placed, Blaine leaned back in his chair. "You're no better than the kidnapper. You're holding the ransom for ransom for what? A shitty meal?"

Bastian looked up. "Listen, mate, we've been working 'round the clock. We barely had time to sleep, let alone eat. Last night, I dragged you out of that car. And that man," he jerked his head toward Mercer, "saved your life. We could have driven away and left you to die, but we didn't. Lord help us, we'll do whatever we possibly can to rescue your son. That isn't a question. The only question that needs answering is what's on this drive. Frankly, I'm tired of the deception. Just answer the bloody question."

"Government files." Blaine traced the wood pattern on the laminate desk. "Specifically evaluations of Darkfire's performance, personnel files, proposed troop movements, the intel they collected, everything pertaining to them and their people."

"Isn't that classified? Not the corporate bullshit, but the intel they've divulged concerning hostiles in the area?"

"I'm a senator."

"That wouldn't have granted you unfettered access. Not to this. Not condensed into a single unit."

"I was part of a committee that reviewed our actions and involvement and ultimately decided against the use of PMCs. This information was presented to us in a closed hearing."

"And they gave out copies as party favors?" Bastian cocked an eyebrow.

"No." Blaine went back to staring at the desk.

"You stole it because you were afraid it would implicate you." Bastian looked at Mercer. "I'm getting really sick of you always being right. Aren't there any decent human beings left in this world?"

"Bas," Mercer feared his friend might become untethered if allowed to dwell too long on the point, "it's of no concern."

Sighing, Bastian nodded. "How do I access the files?"

"Why? You don't need them. You don't need to see them." Blaine stared at the analyst. "Why can't you just let it be?"

"Because unlike you, I won't sell out your government or your troops." Bastian spun the computer around. "Enter your access key."

"I don't have it."

"Convenient."

"I'm serious. I don't. A new key is generated every fifteen minutes. The device that creates that key is locked in my office in Washington. I can't access these files, and neither can anyone else."

"Where there's a will." Bastian cycled through a bevy of programs and algorithms.

"Even if you could break into it, you can't alter the files. Wolf will know. He'll kill Nathaniel. He wants the drive to cover up Darkfire's actions and involvement. Maybe he wants it to hide his own guilt." Blaine's protest was valid, but Mercer didn't believe that was the only reason Blaine wasn't cooperating.

"Tell us why you're afraid. Now." Mercer stood over Blaine, a hand on his shoulder. He felt a tremble go through the senator.

"Opening that database will create an automatic connection to the government server. Once that happens, it can be traced. Someone at the DOD or NSA will know. These things are monitored. They'll realize it was me. It's my code."

"They already know what you've done." Mercer released the senator. "Bas, finish up here. Are Donovan and Hans set up like we planned?"

"Isn't it a bit early?"

"That won't be an issue." Mercer passed the room service delivery on his way out. Halting the bellhop, he lifted the lid and snatched a slice of bacon and a muffin on his way to the lift. Bastian wasn't the only one who hadn't eaten lately.

TWENTY-NINE

"You're early." Loren gestured to the empty chair.

"As are you." Mercer eyed their surroundings, catching a glimpse of two agents in the vicinity. "You're not alone."

"Neither are you." The American smiled, reaching for his iced tea with his good hand. His other arm had been properly bandaged and placed in a sling. In his linen suit, clean-shaven, and wearing what Julian imagined were regulation aviator sunglasses, the man no longer looked like a vacationing millennial. He now resembled the formidable opponent he was. "At least we're finally being honest with one another." He placed the glass back on the table, adjusting it before sitting back in the chair. "I am not your enemy."

"Prove it."

Loren let out a polite laugh. "You're alive. Doesn't that say it all? If I wanted, I could have you killed right now. You'd never see it coming. But I don't want that. And you don't want that."

"Are you certain my men don't have your team in

their sights?"

"Did you really come here to find out whose is bigger? Say the word, and I'll unzip and drop trou so we can get this over with." After a brief stare down, Loren smiled. "Then let's get down to business." He opened the manila folder in front of him. "Senator Harry Blaine's been a bad boy. He was flagged by the DEA when an attorney for one of the biggest cartels made a large contribution to his campaign. Since then, we've been monitoring the senator. Lobbyists pull the strings on the Hill. Money buys the vote, so this story isn't new. However, Blaine wasn't just selling out to big pharma or some corporate giant. He climbed in bed with a cartel and gave them details concerning an ongoing military operation that had been carefully planned and implemented by several intelligence and defense factions. But you already know this."

"Then stop telling me what I know."

"I already did. Have you checked your maps and files? We left a few hints as to where the kidnappers might be. However, we haven't been able to pinpoint their precise location. Wolf and his team are SpecOps trained. They don't stay in one place too long. They avoid all the normal methods of tracking people. They even seem to have some kind of sixth sense when it comes to satellite positions, which I suspect means they have an insider still with Darkfire who has access to our spy satellites' trajectories."

"And?" From his peripheral vision, Mercer could see the agents on the outskirts of the marketplace speaking into their comms and keeping a visual on the exchange. That meant Loren had at least one sniper in the area. "What do you want from us? We are kidnapping and ransom specialists. This isn't our fight."

"Probably not, but I can't allow you to turn over classified intel to the enemy."

"Then we have a problem."

"Can you say with certainty Wolf will deliver Nathaniel Blaine to you?"

"No."

"Are you sure the boy is alive?"

"As of eight hours ago, he was."

"You received proof of life?" Loren removed his sunglasses to allow Mercer to look into his eyes. This wasn't a bluff or a game of wits. "We might be able to determine the location from the footage. May I see it?"

"What is your mission objective?"

"I'm not at liberty to say."

"Fancy that. We aren't on the same side. My people and I are not part of your team." He wondered where Hans and Donovan were set up. Surely, one of them had eyes on this tête-à-tête. "Once you have a location, you'll go in hot. I won't allow you to jeopardize my negotiation or the boy's safety." Mercer stood. "We're done here."

"Sit down." Loren put his glasses back on and nodded to the laser sight on Mercer's chest. "Unless you want to be put down." He swiveled in an exaggerated attempt to look around. "Where are your people when you need them?"

"You don't want to find out." Mercer retook his seat, the annoyance radiating from him.

"I have no interest in allowing harm to come to the boy. To be frank, I don't give two shits about the mercenaries or what they want. My bosses might think differently, but that's beyond the parameters of my current mission. My team and I are focused on the cartel. Their reach is far too broad. They control a senator who is stupid and arrogant enough to think he can sell out his own people and not get caught. Blaine gave them unbridled access to resources in the Middle East and allowed them to inject themselves into supplying insurgents with heavy artillery. We can't stand by any longer and allow this to continue."

"Are you planning to kill Blaine?"

"Don't be absurd. I don't run a kill team. Sanctioned hits are a thing of the past, at least the ones that are on the books. Blaine's actions will be investigated and evaluated for fallout before any official action is taken against him. Now, if he had been killed by the kidnappers, that would have been a different story, but he's safe, thanks to you. You saved us the trouble of mounting a rescue. That was much appreciated." His tone remained neutral, leaving Mercer unsure if that last bit was meant to be sarcastic.

"I think I'd prefer the bullet rather than dying of boredom. Get to the bleeding point."

"We're on the same side. We need to work together."

"How?"

"You're waiting for Wolf to phone with a time and location for the exchange. We know he's been in contact with the head of the cartel, but we aren't sure how. We need to find out, get a location, and neutralize the threat."

"Why are they working together? Shouldn't they be enemies?" Mercer asked.

"We believe Wolf brokered a deal with the cartel after the police took Lamb into custody. Both sides are allied against Blaine for fear he will be interrogated and forced to sell them out after the ransom is delivered. It's about self-preservation. The PMCs get paid, and the cartel retains control of the region. Obviously, Wolf will have to deliver the ransom to his master, and when he does, we can take them down."

"You want to piggyback off my mission?"

"It's the only way."

"No."

"You know asking is only a courtesy," Loren said. "Not to mention, I can't allow you to turn over sensitive intelligence."

"If I can't deliver the ransom, there won't be an exchange. Wolf will not alter his demands. The boy is dead, and that is on you."

"There's always another way. Our experts can create realistic facsimiles once you hand over the genuine article. We'll give you the fakes, which we will equip with undetectable tracers. You rescue the boy and save the day. My people will follow the cheese back to the rat's nest. We get the cartel. You get the boy. We both get what we want." He flipped the file around and shoved it in front of Mercer. "These are the details we extracted from the man you know as Theodore Lamb."

"The Butcher," Mercer corrected.

"Right, you had a run-in with these cowboys several years ago. After reading through your military record, courtesy of our alliance with the British government, I was surprised you'd work for a prick like Blaine."

"We don't always pick our clients."

"Maybe you should start." Loren stood. "Peruse the information and think about my offer. Wolf will be phoning shortly, and it'll take time to make the ransom look realistic. The more time you waste, the less likely our plan will succeed."

"And if I say no?"

"You won't. Let's stop pretending. We both know you don't have a choice. I will get this done with or without your help. It'd go better for Blaine's family if you're on board."

"Fine."

"Great." Loren lifted a radio from his jacket. "Release his teammate and get started on cloning the tech. We need to be ready to go at any moment."

"What have you done?"

"Don't worry, we're nicer than you are. We didn't break Mr. Clarke's arm." Loren leaned in closer. "Your computer whiz would need that to work the keyboard, but if you get in my way again, I will take my revenge on you." He buttoned his jacket. "Nice chatting with you, Mr. Mercer. I'll be seeing you again real soon."

"Bloody Yanks."

THIRTY

"They've been monitoring the senator. They knew we had a meeting. They knew about the room service. They had their people planted in the hotel, probably since the senator checked in. Maybe even before that." Bastian squeezed the bridge of his nose. "They have the hard drive and the disk. The bodyguards were in on it. I imagine they're spooks too, and the profiles I found were planted just in case someone was dumb enough to look."

"We'll get you a dunce cap," Hans offered.

"Thanks." Bastian glared at him. "At least we have the rest."

Mercer placed a finger to his lips, shaking his head. The safe house wasn't safe. Surely, it was bugged. More than anything, they needed to relocate, but without knowing if their gear had been compromised, it wouldn't solve the problem. After this mission, everything would have to be scrapped. They'd need new devices, weapons, and gear. Probably even clothing.

"Did they say anything?" Mercer asked.

"Just your basic introduction while being held at

gunpoint. They had no interest in harming Blaine. They insisted they were there to help, but they were under the impression I wouldn't be compliant. I can't imagine where they might have gotten that idea."

"They started it," Donovan insisted, "and now they expect us to trust them?"

"We don't," Mercer picked up the phone, listening for clicks or crackles of static before replacing the handset, "but they have the ransom. We need them."

"Not necessarily." Hans reached for a sheet of paper and a pen. After scribbling a note, he handed it to Julian.

The tracker hidden inside the blue duffel bag might still be active. By reactivating the monitor and scouting the locations the Americans had suggested, they could stumble upon Nathaniel's location.

"It's worth a shot," Mercer said. "Split up. Move outward from this position. Only land locations. Anything on the water will require far more stealth than we are capable of."

"Aye, sir." Hans palmed a set of keys and tossed another set to Donovan. "Comms on?"

Mercer nodded. "Watch your backs." After the door closed, he studied the various fixtures and light switches. Then he began a physical search for surveillance equipment hidden inside the flat.

"Is there even a point?" Bastian had been poised at the computer, unable to decide what to do. Pushing away from the screen, he crossed the room and sprawled out on the sofa. "Our legs have been cut out from underneath us. We can't do anything without them finding out and screwing us over."

"They interrogated the Butcher."

"So I see." He snagged the file off the table. "Seems light. This must be what wasn't deemed sensitive."

"I agree. I suspect they know precisely where Wolf

is."

"That would seem fair considering they know where we are." Bastian rolled his eyes. "I don't like this. Maybe we should call—"

"No." Mercer's stern voice cut off the suggestion. "We do not compromise our contacts. Understood?"

"Right-o." Placing the file back on the table, Bastian closed his eyes. "How long do you think it'll take before they hand us an unreliable piece of shite to pass off to Wolf?"

"Not too long. They probably already had a copy of the hard drive. I'd wager the delay is to keep us off balance." Mercer stopped what he was doing, his gaze coming to rest on the front door. "Quiet."

Moving like a lion stalking a gazelle, he drew his weapon and positioned himself next to the door. Signaling to Bastian, he remained hidden while his second-in-command aimed at the center of the door before throwing it open. Outside were two dark-colored SUVs and four men.

"Alexander Loren, I presume." Bastian's cold stare came to rest on the two men in the backup vehicle. "I see you brought your wait staff with you. Did they remember my tea this time?"

"Mr. Clarke," Loren plastered a smile on his face, "kindly lower your gun." Bastian's eyes darted to Mercer for a brief second, and the commander nodded. Holstering his side arm, Bastian stepped away from the door. "Thank you." Loren entered the beachside flat while his entourage remained outside. "Here are the items Wolf requested."

"Demanded." Mercer stepped away from the door, his gun at his side. "Are you positive he won't know the difference between this and the real thing?"

"I had a conversation with my superiors. Wolf wants to know what we have on him and Darkfire, so he shall have it." Loren placed the drive on the table. "As for the disk, let's just say we spent the better part of the afternoon discussing that with Senator Blaine. I believe this is a reasonable estimate of the materials Wolf is expecting to receive."

"Brilliant." Bastian took the offered disk.

"I'm here to collect the rest," Loren said.

"The rest?" Mercer asked.

"Don't play dumb. I know you aren't as stupid as you look. Blaine said you had documents. Where are they?"

Mercer patted his pockets. "I must have misplaced them."

"Is he always this difficult?" Loren asked Bastian.

"Rather insufferable most of the time. I imagine the two of you are rather alike in that regard."

"Stop wasting my time. You have account numbers, ledgers, and maps. That's what Blaine said."

"Did you torture that out of him?" Bastian asked. "I hate to break it to you, but torture doesn't result in reliable intel."

"No, but it can be cathartic. So don't test me."

"Why would I? We're on the same side, mate." Bastian pointed to the table. "That top folder on the left stack, that's what you're looking for."

"Bas," Mercer said.

"Shut it, Jules. We're out of options." Bastian dropped onto the couch. "Is there anything else we can do for you? Care for a pint? It's about all that's in our fridge. Ask your mates to step inside and join us. We'll make it a party."

Loren opened the file and scanned the pages. "We'll be going now."

The car door had just slammed when the phone rang. "Shite." Mercer lunged for the phone. "Stop them."

Bastian dashed out the door, waving frantically until the SUVs halted. The engines idled while Bastian made his way to the passenger's side. "Wolf's on the line. We're gonna need that intel."

"No way." Loren shook his head. "That's too damn coincidental."

"Coincidence or not, it's happening."

"Bullshit. I knew it was too easy when you handed this over without a fight. You're not getting it back."

"I'm sorry, but I have to insist." Bastian pulled his weapon, shooting out the front and rear tires before aiming at Loren. Three weapons were aimed at his chest, but he didn't back down. "A boy will die without those papers. We don't have time for this."

"Blaine should have thought about that before selling his soul to the devil." Loren blinked a few times. "Fuck." He slammed his fist against the dash. "Stand down. Stand down," he repeated into his radio. He turned to the driver. "Get on the horn and have our tac team prepared to move out." Pressing his lips together, he studied Bastian. "Don't make me regret this, Clarke. You better save the kid. If he dies, I'm gonna kill you."

"Trust me, mate, if this goes pear-shaped, I'll load the gun for you." Taking the documents, Bastian raced back into the house.

Mercer was writing something on a sheet of paper. Seeing Bastian, he folded the paper and hung up the receiver. "It's done. The exchange will take place in one hour. He gave me the coordinates. He wants everything in exchange for Nathaniel, including the rest of the five mill wired to his account."

"I'll grab my gear. Have you radioed Hans and Donovan?"

Mercer shook his head, spotting Loren approaching the house with his team behind him. Waiting for the

Americans to enter, he checked his gun. "You're to remain here. He wants me to come alone."

"The hell you will," Loren protested, catching the end of the conversation. "Not with classified intel. My people will create an invisible perimeter. We'll monitor the area. We'll track them after they leave. They'll never see us, but we'll be there."

"It's too risky."

"I wasn't asking for permission," Loren said. "Tell us, or no one will make it to the exchange."

Mercer moved behind Bastian on his way to the back room, slipping the note into the other man's pocket on the way. A second later, he emerged with a vest and a few extra weapons. "Are you positive they won't spot you?"

"They won't. You have my word," Loren promised.

"Fine. You should set up first. If we arrive together or within close proximity, Wolf might see your convoy and become suspicious. I'm to rendezvous with him in an hour. Here are the coordinates." Mercer wrote down the longitude and latitude. "Do not jeopardize my op. Is that understood?"

Loren nodded. "Good luck."

"You too. Now if you'll excuse me, I need to update my client and have some funds transferred before the exchange." Without another word, Mercer left, snorting at the flat tires on one of the vehicles. Bastian really had a flair for the dramatic. Hopefully, the Yanks had fallen for it.

THIRTY-ONE

"We're playing with fire," Donovan cautioned. "We don't have visual confirmation that Nathaniel is on the premises. Repeat no visual on the package."

"What does the tracker say?" Mercer asked. "Are you certain it's live and active?"

"Yes, sir. Thirty-seven meters from my present location."

"Remain a ghost. Do not engage."

"Aye."

"I'll speak to the senator. Going silent." Mercer muted the mic on his comm and marched into the hotel. Taking the lift to the proper floor, he knocked on the door. When no one answered, he knocked louder. Annoyed by this delay and fearing what the senator's absence might mean, he returned to the lobby. "Where the bloody hell is Senator Harry Blaine?"

"Mr. Mercer, Mr. Blaine left a message for you. The hospital phoned twenty minutes ago. Should you need him, he's with his wife."

Taking the car a few blocks, Mercer pulled into the parking lot, leaving the vehicle at the far end of the emergency lane. Sprinting inside, he dashed down the hallways, aware of the time ticking away. Entering Barbara's room, Mercer didn't expect the scene in front of him.

"She's awake." Blaine smiled brightly. "It's a miracle." Although from the looks of the woman, it didn't appear to be a miracle.

"I need to speak to you. Now." Mercer stepped out of the room.

"Is this about the group of agents the government sent after me? They know," Blaine said. "What are they going to do? Did you tell them? I spent the afternoon being interrogated. I thought they might kill me after I answered their questions, but instead, they said they would help get Nathaniel back."

"Wolf phoned. The exchange will commence in forty-five minutes. He wants everything we agreed to previously, plus an additional 3.4 million Euros. It doesn't need to be cash, but he wants it wired to his account. I need access to your funds."

"Yeah. Okay." Blaine took a pen from his pocket and scribbled down the information. "That should cover it. I don't know what the exchange rate is, but this account should have enough." He held the paper out but refused to let go when Mercer reached for it. "You'll bring Nathaniel home, right?"

"I'll try."

"Do more than that. Agent Loren said he was assisting. Is that true? Didn't Wolf insist you come alone?"

"I'll handle it." Mercer looked at his watch.

"Go." Blaine practically pushed Mercer in the opposite direction. "Save my son."

Dashing back to the vehicle, Mercer reactivated his

mic. "Hans, any sign of the Americans?"

"Negative. Based on the GPS tracker Bastian slipped into Loren's pocket, they went to the decoy location. No sign of them approaching the target's base."

"Any sign of the package?"

"Still no visual," Donovan said. "I have eyes on Lemming, Fox, and Hawke. The Wolf Pack is present."

"What about their leader?" Mercer asked, the tires spitting sand into the air when he turned the wheel too sharply.

"Negative on Wolf," Donovan replied. "He might already be en route to the exchange site."

"Bastian, what's your ETA?" Mercer asked.

"Twenty minutes. Those wankers took longer than necessary to leave. They might be on to us. Jules, should I redirect and meet you at the exchange site instead? We don't have a visual on the boy. He could be in either location."

"Or neither. Maintain your course."

"Hans, are you certain the Wolf Pack is at your location?" Bastian asked.

"Affirmative. At least three of them. Like I said, no visual on Wolf or Bear."

"They must be positioned at that location for a reason," Bastian said. "You're certain this was one of the locations the Americans circled?"

"Not exactly," Donovan responded. "A cargo ship is docked at the wharf the Americans pointed out."

"A ship makes sense." Mercer calculated the likelihood of his team being able to sneak on board without being detected, locate Nathaniel, and escape. "Bas, is it possible the package could be on board, given the last proof of life video we received?"

"Yep. Let's not forget they have liquid assets

available. They could easily pay off a ship's captain to grant them passage without asking too many questions."

"Heads up," Hans interrupted, "there's a fourth player. I can't see his face. Could be Wolf." He blew out a breath. "Fucking turn around."

"I need that identity," Mercer said.

"Hang on, Jules." Hans and Donovan relayed positions and directions to one another, hoping to get a confirmation. "It's Wolf. Repeat we have confirmation on Wolf."

"Nathaniel has to be there," Mercer decided, missing his turn and whipping the car around only to sideswipe the motorist driving behind him. Horns blared, and curses ensued. But it didn't stop him from mashing down the accelerator. "Find a way onto that ship and determine where the boy is being kept."

"I believe I know," Donovan said. "There's a cargo container in the vicinity of the Wolf Pack. It's on the main deck, starboard side toward the rear."

"Civilians?" Bastian asked. "What about the ship's crew?"

"No movement to report. They could be below deck, on the bridge, or in quarters," Hans replied. "What's the plan?"

"How long would it take to get from the ship to the exchange point?" Mercer asked.

"Fifteen minutes, maybe twenty," Bastian guessed.

"They have fifteen minutes until departure if they want to make it on time," Mercer said. "They'll have to bring out the boy. We need to be prepared to take him."

"Jules," Bastian protested, "are you certain you shouldn't wait and see how it plays out?"

"Do you believe Wolf will hold up his side of the agreement?" Mercer asked, knowing an exchange was usually the best and safest way of ensuring the kidnapped victim was recovered.

"Not particularly," Bas admitted.

"Donovan, find a way inside. Hans, continue to serve as overwatch. Report any changes in movement pattern with Wolf's team immediately. If Loren and those shitheads show up, let me know," Mercer said. "Should Wolf take the boy and leave for the exchange, I'll get there before he does."

A set of affirmatives rang out over the comms.

"Make sure you do," Bas said. "I'll be there as soon as I can. I need to make certain I don't have a tail." The unspoken warning came through loud and clear. Their communications could be compromised. Loren and his team could already be aware of the situation and not the diversion Mercer crafted.

After several minutes of utter silence, Hans cursed. "Shit. We have company, and it isn't the Americans. I'm guessing these bastards are with the cartel. Armored vehicles, body armor, and assault rifles."

"How many?" Mercer asked.

"Eight on my side. Donovan, anyone near you?"

"Negative, but I found a way on board. The life raft on the side can be reached via rope. From there, it's straight up to the main deck. It allows a cover position behind several cargo containers. We could use that position to mount a strike."

"We're talking twelve armed hostiles," Bastian reminded the team. "Those aren't good odds."

"I can even them up," Hans offered.

"Hold position," Mercer said. "Where's Wolf?"

"Speaking to one of the new players." Hans sighed. "Another vehicle just arrived with four more hostiles."

"They know we're coming, Jules," Bastian said. "Or they suspect we're planning something. I wonder how many are waiting for you at the exchange."

Mercer slammed the brakes, nearly causing a pile-up behind him. "I best find out." Getting out of the car, he ignored the angered shouts and curses while he hoofed it to the fleabag motel. Not wanting to give the enemy a potential heads-up, Mercer thought it wise to surprise them by arriving on foot.

Outside the motel, he spotted a Land Rover. "They're waiting," he said into his comm. "I'm making the approach now. Should I not make it, find a way to get the package clear, is that understood?"

"Jules, be careful," Bastian said.

Removing his weapon, Mercer held it at his side. His grip was tight, and he fought against his instincts to allow the muzzle to lead. The lights on the vehicle flashed. Before he could say or do anything else, two men got out, weapons aimed at him.

"Do not resist," one of them said.

Without warning, two more men came from behind, firmly grabbing Mercer's arms. He recognized the scent in an instant—sunscreen and cologne. *Damian Bear.* Then a hood was thrown over his head, his weapon confiscated, and he was led forward.

"Step up," one of the men ordered, and Mercer complied, entering the back of the Land Rover. "Wolf wanted to ensure you weren't followed and that you came alone."

"I am alone," Mercer said. "Where are we going?"

"To make the exchange."

"You're taking me to Wolf?" Mercer asked for the benefit of his team.

"Yes." The voice chuckled. "For the record, your team can't hear you. This vehicle is equipped with a jammer. Your radio won't work and neither will your trackers."

Mercer listened for outside noises or sounds indicating they were heading toward the water. He counted the turns in his head, the number of times there was a stop and go, and tried to determine the direction they were traveling. He couldn't be certain, but it seemed things were going as planned. Hopefully, his team would be prepared to mount a rescue if necessary.

THIRTY-TWO

The vehicle came to an abrupt halt, and the hood was ripped off Mercer's head. He looked out at the dilapidated cargo ship in front of him, wondering if it was even seaworthy. Bear sat in front of him, a gun in his hand.

"Do you have the items?"

"Shouldn't you have asked that sooner?" Mercer retorted. Bear continued to glare until Mercer finally answered, "Yes. Do you have the boy?"

"Indeed."

Bear nodded to the man on the left who opened the car door and stepped out. The man on Mercer's right pushed him out of the vehicle. Mercer didn't waste time looking around. He knew their destination. His only concern was whether his team had time to prepare for the exchange.

"Follow me." Bear set off toward the staircase that led to the ship.

As Mercer followed, he noted the way Bear favored his right side. The bullet had done some damage, but

Bear had no intention of showing any weakness. In fact, the man was being nothing but professional. Perhaps there was a chance the exchange would be civil and contingencies would not be necessary.

"Ah, Mr. Mercer," Wolf's voice rang out, "do you have my money and the intel?"

"I want to see Nathaniel."

"Do you now?" Wolf stepped out from the darkened shadow of the bridge. The cargo ship was so old the bridge didn't even have doors. The windows were broken, and the few that remained were caked with grime. "I wasn't aware you were in charge. I'm fairly certain I'm the captain of this ship, and what I say goes. Watch this." He smiled sadistically and spoke Portuguese or some dialect of Spanish with which Mercer wasn't entirely familiar. The three armed men cocked their weapons and aimed at Mercer. "I suggest you don't move too quickly."

"Kill me and the money is forfeit. Only I have the account number and access codes." He tapped his forehead. "They're right here."

"It would almost be worth it," Wolf said. "Don't you agree, Damian?"

Bear didn't speak. Instead, he maintained his dead-eye stare.

"Is the package unharmed?" Mercer sensed the theatrics would only get worse until the situation escalated to violence.

"Nathaniel is alive. For how long is up to you." Wolf gestured behind him, and several other armed men opened the door to the cargo container at the far end of the ship. Inside was the cot from the video and a child-sized lump huddled beside it.

"Release him," Mercer ordered.

"You still don't understand who's in charge." Wolf made a hand gesture and another man yanked the boy off the floor, resulting in a blood-curdling scream that was amplified by the echo from the metal container.

Mercer's fists clenched. His breath became shallow, and he saw red. For a moment, he wasn't certain he wouldn't rip out Wolf's throat.

"Jules, we don't have an angle inside the container," Donovan's voice sounded in Mercer's ear, calming the rage. "We're attempting to reposition. There are twenty-one hostiles on board. No civilians have been detected. However, we can't guarantee Nathaniel's safety if this turns into a firefight."

"Stop," Mercer said, his voice strong and forceful. "The boy's well-being is our only priority. Please," he focused on Wolf, "do not hurt him."

"That's more like it." Wolf studied Mercer. "Where's the intel?"

"In my breast pocket."

Bear holstered his weapon before reaching into Mercer's jacket and removing a folded envelope. Inside, the documents were folded around the hard drive and disk. Flattening the sheets, Bear flipped through them. "They need to be verified."

"By all means," Wolf gestured to the bridge, "let's step into my office."

One of the armed men poked Mercer with the muzzle of his gun, pushing him forward. In the contained space, it might be possible to take out Wolf, Bear, and the three armed men without drawing too much attention, but that left sixteen hostiles and the hostage nearly sixty meters away. Those weren't ideal odds.

"Jules," Bastian whispered, "two sentries have been eliminated. Nineteen tangos remain."

"Shit," Hans cursed, "Fox and Hawke are inside the container with Nathaniel. I have no shot. One millimeter outside the container and they're dead, but as long as they are inside that blasted container, there's no angle."

Mercer listened to his team relay details while Bear and Wolf huddled around a computer terminal, comparing the charts and pages to map coordinates. After several interminably long moments, Wolf turned to Mercer.

"You must have hoped to outsmart me." He tapped the external drive. "You didn't realize I already had a copy of the encryption key." He plugged a USB drive into one of the ports, waiting for the intel to present itself. In less than a second, an array of files opened, creating a waterfall cascade on the screen. "They can't touch me now." He turned to Bear. "They can't touch us. We have everything. Our orders, the government approval, the evaluations, internal memos, all of it. They can't blame this shit on us any longer. Darkfire didn't screw up. We didn't screw up." He looked at Mercer, an actual smile on his face. "Bravo. I'm impressed. Now, how about that cash deposit?" Keying in some banking information, he spun the computer toward Mercer. "If you'd be so kind."

"You get paid when the boy is released."

"He'll be free to go once I have my money."

"I'm not an idiot. You've provided zero assurances you will allow us to leave. You are not getting the ransom until I have been granted safe passage away from here with the boy."

Wolf cocked his gun and pressed it against Mercer's forehead. "Who's in charge?"

"Don't be stupid. Do you want the money or not?"

"John," Bear said from beside him, "don't forget our debts. Our original mission was compromised. Our new partner expects restitution. We can't afford to disappoint him."

"Put the keys in the ignition," Mercer said, "and

have the boy taken to the SUV. Once he's inside, I want your men to move away from the vehicle and clear a path between here and there. After that's done, I will enter the account information. You will allow me to leave, and when I make it to the car, I will give you the access code. You get your money, and everyone walks away breathing. That's the only way this goes down."

"I could kill the boy if you refuse to give me the code."

"You've damaged the package already. I would assume any overt threat is more than just a threat, and you get nothing." Mercer glanced at Bear. "A bit of advice, you should listen to your teammate and trust his judgment."

"And where's your team?" Wolf asked. "Are they waiting around that motel for you to return? Is that the kind of trust you were talking about?"

"Wrap this up," Hans said, his voice urgent. "We have company coming. A convoy has just entered the wharf. I assume more cartel soldiers are on the way."

"I know my men. They'll make sure no harm befalls the package through any means necessary."

"Affirmative," Hans replied.

Mercer's only goal was getting the boy clear of the container and into the SUV. Hellfire was about to rain down, and they needed to be clear of this godforsaken rust bucket before that happened.

"Fine," Mercer said, "bring the boy to me. Then I'll give you the money."

"This could go on all day." Wolf sighed. "I have more important things to do than chat anyway." He spoke again in the same foreign language, and the two armed men went to fetch Nathaniel. "The account number." He lowered his gun. "We both just want to get paid, right?"

Mercer reached for the keyboard. Slowly, he pecked away until the account number filled in the first blank. Taking a step back, he allowed Wolf to fill in the transfer amount. While the former PMC was typing, Mercer looked around the room. No weapons were visible, but he was more interested in finding cover positions. The consoles and corners around the navigation equipment might provide a hiding place for someone Nathaniel's size. The thick metal would slow possible gunshots, but given the rust and structural damage, he had little faith it would stop the shot completely. This ship was a deathtrap.

"We have a visual on the boy. He's being escorted by four tangos. Do we engage?" Donovan asked.

"Wait," Mercer said, causing Wolf to look up, "what is my method of safe passage?"

Wolf didn't speak.

"Commander, our window is closing," Donovan said.

"You have no intention of letting us live. You have no qualms about murdering a child?" Mercer turned to Bear. "And you have no bloody say in the matter? Where is your honor?"

Wolf finished entering the amount, turning the screen back to Mercer. "The access code." He cocked his gun, aiming again at Mercer's head.

Bear looked a tad uneasy, and Mercer homed in on it. "You didn't sign up for murdering women and children, did you, soldier? Your CO's lost the plot. He's gone mad, or he was daft from the beginning."

Wolf clocked Mercer with the gun, sending him reeling back a few steps. "Shut your mouth."

Mercer righted himself, pressing a hand to the bloody gash at his brow.

"This is personal. Senator Shithead cost me everything. He cost us everything. Our jobs, our families, everything that was good in our lives he took away in order to line his pockets with gold. Why shouldn't we take everything from him?" Wolf asked.

"Maybe he deserves to suffer, but his son doesn't." The slight double vision started to abate, but one thing was clear, Wolf intended to kill Nathaniel. "You put his wife in a coma. His career is over. His treasonous acts have been exposed." It was a last ditch effort to appeal to Wolf's humanity or possibly Bear's, if the underling was willing to step in and usurp his commander. "No one else needs to die. You have what you want. You have evidence, proof, and enough money to start a new life. It doesn't have to go like this."

"Jules," Bastian's voice jittered, "they'll be on you in five seconds."

"I'll give you the money. Let the boy go," Mercer said.

"Time's up," Bastian whispered.

THIRTY-THREE

Wolf turned as the four men appeared in the doorway with the eleven-year-old sandwiched in the middle. Without blinking, Wolf aimed at Nathaniel. "Start typing."

"Take it easy." Mercer entered several digits, his focus on the scene before him and not the screen.

The boy had been injured, but he was walking upright under his own power. The contusions on his face might have been minor or even cosmetic, but from the howls he emitted earlier, Mercer assumed the worst.

Wolf had his weapon at the ready. He'd be Mercer's priority. Bear's injury would prove useful in slowing his reaction time. That just left the four men clustered around the boy.

"Five, four," Mercer muttered, and Wolf turned to see what he was mumbling about.

Continuing the countdown, Mercer lunged for Wolf's weapon, aiming it skyward. The shot went high, reverberating in the enclosed space while the two cartel soldiers were gunned down. Elbowing Wolf in the face, Mercer spun, keeping a tight grip on the weapon while he delivered a high kick to Wolf's sternum. The man fell backward, and Mercer fired a round into his skull.

A spray of bullets came at Mercer from two directions. He hit the deck. Nathaniel screamed. He had to get to the boy. The sound of sniper fire rang out, and Fox went down. Hawke grabbed the screaming Nathaniel by the waist and disappeared from Mercer's view.

"Get the boy," Mercer barked, taking a strong kick to the ribs that sent his body sliding a few feet across the floor.

He had been distracted long enough for Bear to join the assault, leaving just enough time to look up and see the muzzle of Bear's gun aimed at his chest. Bear squeezed the trigger, following through with the traditional double-tap.

Mercer flopped backward. The world blinked out. He couldn't breathe. He couldn't think. Pain flooded over him, canceling out his senses. Then as suddenly, he gasped, his body coming alive with a flow of adrenaline. The gun he'd been holding had clattered out of reach. His animalistic side took over, and he leapt at Bear, knocking the man's weapon away.

Slamming the PMC into the ground, Mercer focused on the man's injury, hitting the approximate location of the bullet wound until the man screamed in agony. Then Mercer yanked the man's head backward, putting him into a chokehold until all fight left his body.

With the immediate threat removed, Mercer slumped to the side. Tearing at his shirt, he found the vest intact. The bullets lodged in the ceramic plates. Dragging himself to his hands and knees, he took a few shallow breaths and climbed to his feet.

"Where's the package?"

"Hawke is taking him back to the container," Donovan said. "We're trying to slow his progress, but he's using the boy as a shield. We can't get a clear shot."

"Eleven hostiles remain," Bastian said. "I'll run interference and divert fire."

"Bloody hell," Hans swore. "Donovan, are you close to the boy?"

"Negative."

"Bas?" Hans asked, becoming more desperate.

"I'm pinned down."

Stepping out of the enclosed bridge, Mercer saw the carnage unfolding around him. Several bodies littered the deck, and the constant report of gunfire meant the cartel soldiers weren't concerned with running out of ammunition. It was a war zone.

At the far end of the ship, Hawke had Nathaniel by the collar. The PMC crouched beside the boy, holding a machete to the kid's throat. One quick move and he'd lob off the kid's head. Hawke's other arm was snaked around Nathaniel's torso, a gun held in his hand.

Armed with nothing more potent than a handgun, Mercer moved forward, his aim on the man at the end of the deck. Shots rang out from all sides, but Mercer's approach remained steady. He would kill that man or die trying.

"Anyone have a clear shot?" Mercer asked, closing the distance. Hawke eyed him but didn't retreat or flinch. He'd backed himself into a corner, surrounded by the cargo containers. Nathaniel was too terrified to scream, but his fear was evident. "Donovan, can you get atop the containers and take him from behind?"

"I'm on my way." But the uncertainty lingered in

the air.

Ten meters from the target, Mercer slowed his pace. Several frantic rounds of gunfire sounded on the other side of the ship, but he couldn't be distracted with concern for Bastian right now. They had a job to do, and they knew the risks.

"Let him go," Mercer bellowed.

"I do, and you'll shoot me." Hawke's head remained on a swivel. He expected reinforcements to arrive and help him out of this mess. "You're outnumbered. More men will be here any second. Turn around and walk away."

"Not without the boy." Mercer focused the laser guide of the handgun on the man, but from the angle and position, he wasn't certain he wouldn't hit the shaking Nathaniel. "Drop the machete."

"No way." Hawke pulled Nathaniel closer, taking a few steps back. He didn't want to trap himself inside the cargo container, but he wanted to prevent anyone from sneaking up behind him. "On your knees," he growled in Nathaniel's ear, and the boy dropped to all fours.

Before Mercer could fire off a single shot, Hawke fired a burst from the fully automatic weapon. Mercer dove to the side. He couldn't return fire with Nathaniel so close.

"Don't even think about it," Hawke warned. He fired again. A bullet grazed Mercer before he had time to roll out of the way. Hawke pulled the trigger again, but nothing happened. "Dammit." Hawke released the gun, gripping the machete in both hands. He held it up, prepared to deliver a downswing to the back of Nathaniel's neck. "Drop your weapon. Hands in the air. I won't ask again."

"Okay," Mercer held his palms up, "I surrender. I'll give you the money. The codes. Whatever you want.

Just don't do this."

Hawke snorted. "Why would I believe you? You just murdered my associates."

"It's war." Mercer didn't take his eyes off the scene before him. He edged closer. "Shit happens."

"Should I thank you for increasing my cut?"

"That's up to you." Mercer took another tiny step forward.

"Back up," Hawke ordered. "I'm not falling for any more of your tricks." Cries of dying men mixed with the staccato rhythm of gun battle. "Call off your team."

"How?"

"Don't fuck with me. Just do it." When Mercer didn't comply fast enough, Hawke took a practice swing with the blade, coming within a few centimeters of Nathaniel's neck.

"Okay. Everyone, hold fire. We're done."

"I'm almost in position," Donovan said. "Buy me another fifteen seconds."

"I'm not sure I'll be alive and kicking in fifteen seconds," Bastian said.

The sound of gunfire grew louder and then suddenly stopped. Hans had taken out a group of men to Mercer's left with his sniper rifle. Instead of remaining on overwatch, he had boarded the ship, his eye glued to the scope. Muscle memory guided his fingers to reload the weapon while he moved with a level of certainty and stealth from one position to another, hoping to find a vantage point to end this. From what Mercer could tell, Hawke was too focused on the gunfight raging nearby and Mercer's position that he hadn't spotted Hans coming up from behind the crates.

"Shit." Bastian sucked in a sharp breath, and Mercer knew he'd been hurt. "Did anyone tell them to hold fire?"

Hawke chuckled, satisfied at the radio chatter saying the enemy had been subdued. "You really thought I'd let you walk away?" Raising the machete again, Hawke reared back, intending the downward swing to have maximum force.

In that instant, two things happened simultaneously. Donovan fired, punching a hole through Hawke's skull, while Hans raced out of nowhere, throwing himself over Nathaniel to protect him from the blade. Unfortunately, Donovan's shot had come too late. The momentum carried the blade and the now dead Hawke forward, bringing them down on top of Hans.

The guttural scream shook Mercer at an emotional level he no longer believed he was capable of feeling. "Kill them all," Mercer ordered, rushing to the dead mercenary. He threw the man's body to the side. The blade protruded from Hans' shoulder like a knife carving a roast. Blood was everywhere.

"Save the boy." Hans lifted himself high enough off the ground for Mercer to grab Nathaniel. "Go, Jules. Get him clear."

"Shut it," Mercer said. "We're not going anywhere without you." Grabbing the side arm from Hans' thigh holster, Mercer surveyed the area for imminent threats, performing a single kill shot. Then he pressed the boy against his chest. "Close your eyes," Mercer whispered. "You're safe now. We'll get you back to your mum and dad soon enough. I promise."

The kid was wracked with sobs, shaking and damp from who knows how many bodily fluids. Two of the cartel's foot soldiers burst onto the deck from one of the lower levels, and Mercer shot them in rapid succession, his aim spot-on and lethal.

"Bas, you're clear," Donovan reported into the

comms. He dropped down from atop the cargo container. "Shite." He pulled the limited medical supplies from inside his vest pockets. "Hang on, mate. You'll be fine." He nudged Hans' thigh. "Stay with us. Stay awake." Donovan made eye contact with Mercer. "We can't move him until we get the bleeding stabilized, and I don't think we should remove the blade. It might be the only thing keeping his shoulder attached."

Hans' whimpers and groans broke his team's will. "Leave me and get Nathaniel home. That's our objective," Hans managed through gritted teeth. He started to convulse, and Donovan pulled out a syringe and jammed it into his teammate's leg.

"That ought to take the edge off." Donovan swallowed, knowing Hans was no longer coherent. "He's going into shock. Why the bloody hell didn't we recruit a combat medic when we took off on our own?" The medical supplies he carried in his pack weren't going to cut it. "This isn't our normal crisis." He tried to wrap the bandage around the blade from shoulder to shoulder to keep Hans in one piece until they could get actual help.

Bastian swore, coming up behind them and nearly becoming a casualty of Mercer's hypersensitivity. "My god."

"Bas, take Nathaniel and get the bloody hell away from here." Mercer passed the child he was cradling to Bastian. "Go."

"Jules, another convoy just arrived." Bas nodded toward the dock where another two SUVs had just pulled up. "Either we all leave, or no one does." He looked at Donovan. "You'll need my help to carry him out of here."

Donovan shook his head. "He won't make it, and I'm not leaving him."

"Take the boy and get clear. That's an order," Mercer said.

"Jules," Bastian protested.

"Move your arse, Clarke."

Bastian took Nathaniel in his arms as several masked men dressed in black stormed the cargo ship. A few echoes of the word clear sounded as they split up, entering the bridge and various other areas. Several men continued on their path toward the kidnapping specialists.

"Whoa," the lead officer released the grip on his gun, letting it hang against his side as he raised his palms, "we're here to help. Mercer," the man yanked the ski mask upward to expose his face which Julian recognized from his encounter with Loren, "we've been informed of the situation. Sir," he took a tentative step forward, "it appears you could use a hand."

Lowering the weapon, Mercer nodded. "We need a med evac."

"Medic," the man yelled. He reached for the radio and ordered a helo to take them to the nearest military hospital.

THIRTY-FOUR

Mercer rubbed his eyes and turned his attention to the man lying in the hospital bed. In the last fourteen hours, Hans had undergone two surgeries. He'd lost a lot of blood, but the doctors had saved his arm, reattaching several tendons and ligaments. As of yet, they had no way of knowing how successful their interventions had been. The reconnaissance expert would be facing a long, hard road to recovery.

"Jules," Bastian rasped from the chair beside him, "any changes?"

"No." Mercer looked at the analyst, seeing Bastian's leg propped up against the foot of Hans' bed. "How are you feeling?"

"Groggy. Whatever pain meds they have, we should ask for samples." He'd been shot in the thigh during the siege, but it had been entirely muscle. Minus the scar, there would be no lasting damage.

"Then get some sleep," Mercer said. "I'll take this shift."

Bastian slid lower in the chair, closing his eyes.

Donovan glanced over at the commander. "Are you going to fight me for it?" he teased. "You don't even like Hans. You don't have to stay."

Julian's icy glare said it all.

"On a serious note, you need to speak to the Blaines. Agent Loren had them moved to this hospital following the debacle on that cargo ship. They'll want to know what happened."

"No, they won't. Bastian already spoke to the senator. That's enough."

"It isn't, and you know it." Donovan leaned forward and stared at his unconscious friend. "We fucked up. It's his dominant arm. His gun arm. What if he can't recover? We need him. Our team needs him. Our job, our new mission in life, whatever it is, we can't do it without him. This shouldn't have happened." He rubbed his eyes. "Bas was hit. He could have easily been killed. You should be dead three times over by now."

"Infinitely more than that."

"Probably so." Donovan laughed. "Who would have thought a concussion would be the best case scenario? I guess I won. Cheers, mate. Drinks will be on me for the foreseeable future." He stood, the movement sobering his thoughts. "We can't carry on without his skill set. Things were dicey enough with the four of us on site. We'd never have made that recovery with a team of three."

"I know."

"Then what are we going to do?"

Mercer didn't have an answer. It was dependent on Hans' condition.

A faint knock sounded at the door, and Mercer looked up. Alexander Loren stepped inside, surveying the wounded. "May I have a moment?" he asked.

Mercer followed the American out of the room.

"Thank you for saving his life."

"Call it professional courtesy. You realize if you had trusted my team instead of sending us in the wrong direction, some of this could have been avoided."

"Your goal was bringing down the cartel. You weren't tasked with assisting on the recovery."

"Well, it wasn't exactly my job, but we see how that turned out." Loren shook his head. "I'm not here to fight. From the looks of things, I'd say we're finally even for the broken arm."

"Fine."

Loren put his palm against Mercer's sore chest. "I wasn't finished. The evidence you turned over, along with what we recovered from the cargo ship, has led to a swift and silent takedown of the cartel's leadership. Senator Blaine's association with the criminal element has been eliminated. However, the cartel itself is vast. Someone else will assume control, but they won't be able to use the American government or our war on terrorism as a means to fund or transport their illegal enterprises."

"That's not my concern."

"I just thought you'd want to know you did something good here. Something much larger than saving an eleven-year-old boy from a group of sadists. In case you were wondering if it was worth it, it was."

"I don't care."

"Perhaps you don't. However, your actions warrant some compensation, so whatever medical assistance you need, we'll provide it." Loren stared at Mercer for a long moment. "We took the liberty of removing your presence from the island. We've arranged temporary accommodations for you and your team. Your belongings are waiting in your quarters. The Blaines will remain on base until the boy has been thoroughly evaluated. We thought it best to remove them before they could be targeted by any remaining factions working with the cartel."

"You mean the police."

"Among others."

Mercer pushed past Loren, reaching for the door handle. Deciding on asking a final question, he turned. "What's to become of the senator?"

"A team of analysts will evaluate the damage he caused and conduct an assessment of the fallout should official charges be brought against him. It's not my call."

Mercer nodded, twisting the knob.

"One last thing," Loren called, "did you drain Blaine's account to pay the ransom?"

"Why?"

"It's drug money. If it's there, it will be confiscated, along with any questionable assets Blaine may have. Even if we allow him to get away with his crimes, we won't let him keep the ill-gotten gains."

"No matter." Mercer rejoined his team, closing the door behind him, but his thoughts were focused on Barbara and Nathaniel Blaine. They'd need substantial funds to support their recovery.

"What was that about?" Donovan asked.

"I'm not entirely certain. Wake Bastian and tell him to find a computer terminal. I'll be right back."

Mercer exited the hospital room in search of the Blaines. After several turns, he came upon their room. He knocked gently, nodding to the soldiers stationed beside the door. Either Blaine was to be protected, or he was under arrest. The precise distinction was impossible to determine.

Blaine came to the door, a large smile on his face. He hugged Mercer as if he were a long-lost brother. "Thank you. Those words don't seem big enough. But thank you."

"How is your son?" Mercer could see the boy curled up against his mother, the two asleep in the bed.

"The doctors are more concerned with the psychological impact than his physical injuries. When you brought him in, he was dehydrated. They did some x-rays. He has four broken ribs and a fractured ulna." Blaine stared at the ground. "I should have never let them separate us. I should have done something to stop them."

"You would have been outmatched."

"I heard about your man. Hans, right? Is he...?"

"It's too soon to tell the extent of the damage."

"I owe him everything. If there's anything we can do, please let me know."

"What is your wife's prognosis?"

"She'll need a lot of rehab and care. Right now, she's paralyzed from the waist down. She only has limited movement in her right arm, and she can't speak." He blinked rapidly, and Mercer wondered if the man was about to break down in tears. "I don't know who will care for her if I'm no longer in the picture. Nathaniel's gonna need counselors and psychiatrists. Honestly, we all do."

"That will require funds. Resources." Mercer wondered if Blaine realized his bank account would be zeroed out. Perhaps he had other assets, like stocks or real estate.

"I'm not complaining. There's no such thing as a free lunch, right?" Blaine offered a half-hearted smile. "Everything's changed overnight. Please extend my sincerest gratitude to your team, Hans in particular. And Mr. Mercer, I need to apologize for accusing you of letting this happen. I was angry and afraid and needed someone to blame besides myself."

"Understood." Giving the family another quick glance, Mercer quietly excused himself.

Returning to his team, he found Bastian upright with a laptop propped on the tray table. Closing the door, he checked the room for surveillance equipment. As soon as he was satisfied they weren't being monitored, he updated Bastian and Donovan on the situation.

"You want me to transfer Blaine's dirty money into an untraceable account?" Bastian shook his head as if he didn't hear the request correctly.

"Yes."

"Jules, I'm fairly certain that's illegal."

"The money was for the ransom. If Wolf had gotten it, it'd be gone now. And as soon as the U.S. government starts poking around in Blaine's accounts, it'll disappear."

"So we're going to steal it?" Donovan asked.

"No, we're going to hide it. That boy and his mum will need every cent to get well."

"And given the laws in the U.S., profits made through illegal means are forfeit." Bastian rubbed a hand down his face. "Do you think they're going to wipe out the Blaines' assets?"

"They might. Loren alluded to as much, but the bloody spook is brilliant with the double-talk." Mercer glanced at Hans who had yet to wake up.

"It'd be nice to have something squirreled away to pay for his expenses should the need arise," Donovan added, following Mercer's gaze. "I say we do it. The money's already dirty. Handing it over to a group of politicians won't make it any cleaner. At least this way, it'll be used for good."

"It's thievery." Bastian tapped anxiously against the tray table. "It's another line we shouldn't cross." Despite his words, he keyed in the information, checking to see if the account had any remaining funds. "I'll do it, but this goes for good. It's not to pay our bar tabs. Agreed?"

"Aye," Donovan said, and Mercer nodded.

"Do I get a vote?" Hans croaked, and all eyes turned to him. "Because you have no idea how much I owe."

"Hans," Mercer moved to stand over the man, "what the bloody hell were you thinking?"

"Is Nathaniel okay?"

"Yes. He's with his mum. Blaine personally thanked you."

"Goody. He bloody well should. The bastard nearly destroyed his family." Wincing, Hans stared at the extensive bandaging along his shoulder and across his chest. "Should I be worried that I can't feel anything?"

"No worries, mate," Bastian said. "The painkillers are topnotch."

Hans didn't speak, reading the worried expressions on Mercer's and Donovan's faces. "Am I dying?"

"No." Donovan cleared his throat. "You'll be okay."

"Jules?" Hans stared at the commander, waiting for the truth.

"Your arm was nearly lobbed off. Future functions might be impaired." Mercer retook his seat beside the bedside. "It's too soon to tell. The docs need to wait for the inflammation to decrease before they can accurately evaluate the nerve damage."

"Wanking might be out of the question," Hans smirked, "but birds dig injured blokes. This ought to really up my game. I'll be getting plenty of action." He glanced around the dingy hospital room. "Tell me, how are the nurses here?"

"Your nurse is a two hundred pound soldier with a crew cut," Bas retorted, clicking away at the keyboard with one hand while continuing to tap anxiously with his free hand.

"She could be worse," Hans decided.

"She's a he," Donovan replied. "And speaking of, someone needs to examine you while you're awake." He left the room to go in search of medical staff.

"Bas, hurry it up," Mercer said.

"It's already done." Bas looked at the two men. "I still don't like it, but we do what we have to in order to save the mark and each other."

"Right-o." Hans winced, reaching for the morphine button with his functioning arm. "If it's all the same to you, I'm going back to numbing bliss." He pushed the button until it refused to dispense any more drugs, and he relaxed, sinking back into the pillow.

THIRTY-FIVE

"Everything's been cleared out." Bastian assessed the scrap heap of destroyed tech that filled several boxes. "We'll finish the decontamination process once we're home."

Mercer nodded. The last place he wanted to go was England. He had sworn not to return to London until he had gotten revenge on his wife's killer, but Hans was hurt. His team was a man down. They had to hole up somewhere to lick their wounds.

Hans wanted to be close to his own mum and in a familiar environment. The doctors estimated it would be six months of intensive physical therapy before he'd regain fifty percent of his motor function and arm strength, so the team would be stationary for the duration, avoiding most jobs that proved difficult or dangerous.

Mercer hadn't even considered finding a replacement, temporary or otherwise. He trusted his team. They had served together under Her Majesty, and they had a bond that couldn't be broken. They wouldn't sell each other out, unlike Wolf and his men who seemed more concerned with themselves than anyone else.

Thankfully, the Americans had been kind enough to provide transport, so Mercer, Bastian, and Donovan packed up whatever belongings remained. Hans had been prepped for transport, and one of the cutting edge facilities in Stanmore was prepared to take him. Everything was set, but it would be odd to be home.

"Did you ever return my lighter?" Bastian asked.

Mercer turned. "What?"

"You borrowed it to light up the senator's car. Did you return it?"

"I don't know."

Bastian rolled his eyes. "In that case, you owe me another bloody Zippo. And the next time you want to light a car on fire with it, the answer is no."

"Why do you need a lighter? You quit smoking," Donovan said, joining the conversation.

"It's the principle of the thing."

"Fine. I'll replace your lighter," Mercer promised.

"Very good." Bastian smiled, taking another moment to check that they'd done everything. "It's odd not cleaning up after ourselves. We left that hotel room and the beach house without executing any of our normal precautions. Do you think the Americans will use it against us?"

"Loren might," Mercer said. "He's playing some game. I just don't know what it is."

"I don't think we're part of it," Donovan said. "He was tasked with containing the situation with the senator. We were just collateral damage."

"Speaking of," Bastian took a seat on the neatly made bed, rubbing the bandage on his leg, "I heard they returned home today."

"Indeed," Mercer said.

"Did you give them access to the transferred funds?"

"No. We'll wait and see what happens before we act. That moron Blaine would probably blab to the wrong person and have the money confiscated."

"Do you think he'll be charged with treason?" Donovan asked.

"Doubtful. Factions within the government like having blackmail to hold over politicians. It's one way to ensure they vote properly and make the right decisions," Bastian said cynically. "I suspect whatever agency employs Loren now controls Blaine. It'll be more advantageous to them to use him than destroy him. Plus, he'll get the sympathy vote on his next reelection campaign. If the senator plays his cards right, he'll be around for a long time."

"It's bloody sickening." Donovan hefted several bags of gear. "I'll go keep Hans company until we're airborne. Someone needs to save the female military personnel from his constant requests for a sponge bath."

Once Mercer and Bastian were alone, Julian took a seat on the adjacent bed. He was exhausted. Rubbing a hand against his sternum, he winced, wondering how long it would be before the bruises went away.

"You never let the docs take a look at you," Bastian mused.

"There was no need."

"Right. I forgot. It's because you don't have a heart. Unfortunately, Jules, you've proven once again that you do." Bas inhaled deeply. "So we're returning to London."

"Yes."

"Are you okay with that decision?"

"It's for Hans. The rest doesn't matter."

Bastian scratched his head and gnawed on an

energy bar. "You phoned Alexis Parker."

"She's FBI. We needed intel on Loren."

"That wasn't the first time you found an excuse to contact her since we helped her out of a jam. I know she's working on finding a lead in Michelle's murder. Does she have anything yet?"

"No." Mercer sat up, annoyed with the turn the conversation had taken. "I don't expect she ever will."

"But you hope so."

"I gave up on hope long ago. It's a four letter word." He slammed the door behind him.

Grumbling to himself, Bastian found a clean burner phone he'd gotten from the exchange and punched in the familiar number. After several rings, the call was answered. "Greetings, love."

"Bastian?" Parker asked.

"The one and only. Any word on Senator Blaine?"

"He gave a press conference this afternoon, thanking everyone for helping rescue his family from terrorists. Apparently, that's the spin they're using. The rogue Darkfire contractors are being viewed as homegrown terrorists. The two who survived, Bear and Lamb, are in custody, being questioned as we speak. I'm just thankful I don't have to deal with it."

"What about the senator and his family?"

"It's too soon to tell, but everything's being kept under wraps. It looks like a CIA cover-up, but what do I know?"

"Plenty." The flirtation came as second nature. "I'm calling for a favor."

"Another one?" Parker sounded hesitant and a bit afraid.

"It's nothing like that," Bastian reassured. "Jules can't be jerked around when it comes to uncovering his wife's killer. And I know you would never intentionally do that, but you have spoken to him on a few occasions when you've needed access to files and other materials."

"Yeah."

"You should know our team will be stationed in London for quite some time. So should the need for extensive legwork arise, I'll make myself available to you. Just give me a call, and I'll handle it. Jules doesn't need to know about this until we have something concrete."

"Okay."

"Thanks, love. You take care."

"You too."

Bastian had just pocketed the phone when Mercer returned. Tossing a small silver package at his second-in-command, he settled back onto the bed. "I don't want to hear about your bloody lighter again."

"Thanks, mate." Bastian flicked the switch, watching the fire erupt from the end. Smiling, he put it back in his pocket. "You didn't happen to pick up some cigarettes, did you?"

"You quit."

"I know, but there's no better way to test out a Zippo, unless there's a wrecked car to light up."

"Shut it." Mercer didn't even bother opening his eyes. "Once Hans is settled and some time has passed, we'll have a special delivery sent to the Blaines. The docs said the facility Barbara transferred to is top of the line. They imagine she'll regain her verbal ability, but until then, her treatment will be expensive, as will Nathaniel's counselors, child care, security details, and who knows what else."

"Like I said, Jules, you've proven once again you have a heart."

"Sod off."

* * *

Several weeks later, Mercer made a couple of phone calls. The money in that account was redirected to several smaller accounts. Taking the extra steps might have been pointless, but he wanted to ensure it remained hidden from the U.S. government. After establishing a fund via anonymous donor, he made sure Barbara and Nathaniel wouldn't have any reason to worry, even if Harry ended up behind bars or dead.

Next, Mercer transferred some of the additional funds into a separate account to cover the treatments Hans would need. His tactician remained in good spirits, despite the circumstances, and the rest of the team held out hope he'd be back to his old self soon enough. They needed him. Those kidnapped victims needed him.

Lastly, Mercer hid the remaining funds in a numbered account that only his team could access. Bastian wasn't pleased, and he voiced his opinion on it numerous times. But the truth of the matter was in most ransom situations, money was always an object. This would give them some wiggle room in negotiations. Plus, it would go a long way toward replacing the gear they had destroyed or lost on this last mission. They'd recover from this. There were no other options.

Subversion

REPARATION, THE NEWEST JULIAN
MERCER NOVEL, IS NOW AVAILABLE IN
PAPERBACK AND AS AN E-BOOK

ABOUT THE AUTHOR

G.K. Parks is the author of the Alexis Parker series. The first novel, *Likely Suspects,* tells the story of Alexis' first foray into the private sector.

G.K. Parks received a Bachelor of Arts in Political Science and History. After spending some time in law school, G.K. changed paths and earned a Master of Arts in Criminology/Criminal Justice. Now all that education is being put to use creating a fictional world based upon years of study and research.

You can find additional information on G.K. Parks and the Alexis Parker series by visiting our website at
www.alexisparkerseries.com